ODD GODS

ODD GODS

BY DAVID SLAVIN
AND DANIEL WEITZMAN

ILLUSTRATED BY
ADAM J.B. LANE

HARPER
An Imprint of HarperCollins*Publishers*

Odd Gods

 For information address HarperCollins Children's Books, a division of HarperCollins Publishers, 195 Broadway, New York, NY 10007.
www.harpercollinschildrens.com
Library of Congress Control Number: 2018964870
ISBN 978-0-06-283953-4
Typography by Andrea Vandergrift
19 20 21 22 23 PC/LSCH 10 9 8 7 6 5 4 3 2 1
❖
First Edition

For Bari—goddess of wisdom, love, and support.
—D.S.

For Elliot.
—A.J.B.L.

For my fellow Odds, especially Zoe and Jonas.
—D.W.

Keep going . . . keep going . . .

Yeah, now we're talking! But higher!

WHOA!!!
Too far!

CHAPTER 1

Look! High up in the sky . . .

Higher . . .

Come back. That's it. Back back back back back—

STOP!!!

We're here.

Mount Olympus. Home of the Greek Gods. And who rules this ancient land?

I do.

I . . . am great.

I . . . am powerful.

I . . . am master of all I survey.

I . . . am a God.

I . . .

"ODDONIS! WAKE UP! YOU'LL BE LATE FOR SCHOOL!!!"

. . . am dreaming.

"ODDONIS! GET UP!!!"

First day of school—also known as WORST day of school. Seriously, does anybody like it? They should just skip the first day and start school on the second day. Only I guess the second day would then be the first day, and everyone would hate the second day, so what's the point?

"ODDONIS!!!!!"

Time to get up. And yes, you heard right: *Odd*onis. Not *A*donis. That's my brother. And no, I'm not the ruler of this ancient land. I'm not great. I'm not powerful. I'm not master of all I survey . . . whatever that means. And I'm not a God. Not really. I'm . . .

. . . a little different.

. . . a little strange.

Let me explain.

FLASHBACK!

The Mount Olympus Hospital Maternity Ward.

That's my mom: Freya. Nordic Goddess of love.

And see the guy pacing back and forth, talking to himself?

That's my dad: Zeus. Greek God of . . . like, everything.

You could say we're a blended family. (More mixed-up than blended, if you ask me.) You could also say my dad is just about to lose it, because he and Mom are about to have a baby!

And look! The baby is born! Oh, and he is *beautiful*, isn't he?

Total Greek God material.
A real Adonis.
So, they named him—what else?—Adonis.
Mom's happy. Dad's happy.
All good, right?
But wait! There's more!
Oh, baby! Another baby!
Hellooooo! Anybody there?
HEY! GET ME OUTTA HERE!!!

And a *second* baby is born! A twin! A boy! Oh, and he is . . .

. . . umm . . .

. . . uhhh . . .

. . . well . . .

Me.

Not exactly Greek God material.

Dad looks at me, looks at Mom, looks back at me, looks back at Mom, and says . . .

"THIS IS *YOUR* FAULT!"

Hmmm. (Personally, I think I looked kinda cute!)

And so they named me—what else?—Oddonis.

FLASH FORWARD!

YIKES! I kind of wish I hadn't flashed forward. I'm staring in the mirror, and this is what I see looking back at me.

And it's a bigger YIKES than usual, because today isn't just any old first day of school. It's the first day of MIDDLE SCHOOL. A new school. A new year. And hopefully, a new *start*.

Some of you might be asking, "Why a new start, Oddonis?" Others of you might be asking, "Why a third nipple, Oddonis?" Well, I can't help you with the nipple, but I can tell you about the new start.

FLASHBACK! AGAIN!

Here I am in grade school. Spartacus Elementary School, to be exact. I'm probably in first grade. (Still think I'm kinda cute!) Awww—and I'm playing in a sandbox, right? Well, not for long. Look what happens next.

There's my brother and his God friends, "digging" what they've done. That's how life rolled in grade school. The Gods pretty much did whatever they wanted, while the rest of us who weren't Gods got . . . buried. On Mount Olympus, it's all about the Gods. Gods, Gods, Gods.

Everybody knows about the Gods and all their amazing powers. But what most mortals don't know is that there's a whole bunch of us on Mount Olympus who aren't really Gods!

Some of us have weak powers, or weird powers, or powers nobody wants, or no powers whatsoever. And others—like, say, for example, ME—have *no idea* what our power is, or if we even *have* a power. Believe me, I've tried to figure that one out for a long, long time. So far, it's basically been a process of elimination.

Here's what I know I'm not:

I'm not strong.

I'm not athletic.

I'm not artistic.

And you know what *really* doesn't help? My brother is ALL THAT!!!

STRONG!

ATHLETIC!

ARTISTIC!

AND he's the God of beauty and desire? WHY??? It isn't fair. Adonis gets everything, and me? Not so much! That's why I'm hoping middle school is a new start. Three grade schools—Spartacus, Zorba, and Troy—all lead to Mount Olympus Middle School, so you get three times more kids. That means more kids who are Gods (like my brother), but more kids who *aren't* Gods, too (like me)! Look, I know it's school, and I know we're not EVER supposed to be excited for school, but today I think I kind of am.

WHOA—and if I don't hurry, I'm going to be late!

One thing I *really* like about the first day of school: Mom always makes a big breakfast—Greek yogurt, Greek omelets, Greek toast (okay, it's French toast, but Dad insists we call everything Greek). Mom's probably the worst cook in the world, but this is her best meal of the year! So you can imagine my disappointment when I get down to breakfast, and all I see are my dad and brother with very full tummies, and a whole pile of very empty plates.

"You snooze, you lose, son!" says my dad.

"You sleep, you weep, little brother!" says my NOT BIG BROTHER. (He was only born like *two seconds* before me!)

"I'm sorry you missed breakfast, sweetie," says my mom, "but you shouldn't have slept so late. I've got a special surprise for you, though: fiskesuppe!"

Fiskesuppe is Norwegian for "fish soup." It's basically a bunch of fish guts mixed in with some twigs and roots. There's even eyeballs in there! And my mom LOVES it! She makes a big pot of it every morning. She also *burns* it every morning. Nothing like starting the day with burnt twigs and fish guts!

"I'm not really hungry, Mom," I lie. I'M ACTUALLY SO HUNGRY!!!

"You have to have breakfast," says Mom, ladling fiskesuppe into my bowl.

"Most important meal of the day," says Dad from behind his newspaper.

Meanwhile, my soup is staring at me.

Then, out of nowhere, Adonis actually does me a favor. He winks at me and says to Mom, "No time, Ma! School chariot's coming!"

"Sorry, Mom!" I say, and grab a NutriGreek bar for the road.

"Let's roll, little bro," Adonis says. "Time for me to *destroy* middle school!"

Dad puts down his paper and says to Adonis, "You know what I expect, son."

"You got it, Pops!"

"What *Olympus* expects."

"Yes, sir! Perfection, sir!"

"Precisely. Go get 'em, tiger!"

Mom rolls her eyes. I wait for Dad to say something to me, but he doesn't, so I say to him, "How about me, Dad? What do you expect from me?"

"You?" asks my dad, furrowing his brow. Then he looks at me, stammers a bit, and says, "Just . . . *try,* Oddonis—that's all anyone can ask."

Hmmm.

Adonis and I grab our backpacks and walk out to the corner to wait for the school chariot. I'm still a little shaken by what my dad said back there, but I'm pretty happy that my brother did me a solid at breakfast. Who knows? Maybe this is the start of a new relationship for us. Maybe we'll become not just twin brothers, but best friends, too!

"Hey, Oddy," Adonis says to me. "Go stand behind that tree until the chariot comes. I don't want anyone to see us together."

Or . . . maybe not.

The yellow school chariot arrives. I wait until Adonis gets on, then I slink out from behind the tree and hop on after him. The most depressed-looking chariot driver I've ever seen greets me. He looks like he's about to cry.

"I'm Phaethon, your driver," he mutters mournfully. "My father is Helios, the Sun God. He granted me one wish, and I asked to drive his sun chariot across the sky. He said it would be too much for me. I said it wouldn't be, but it was, and I crashed. As punishment, I'm doomed to drive this school chariot for all eternity. Take a seat."

BUSINESS IN THE FRONT

Okaaaay. I take a quick glance around the chariot. It's all business in the front—everyone's staring straight ahead, no one's talking—but it's a party in the back. That's where the Gods are. I look closer and see that they've piled all their backpacks across one of the rows of seats, so only Gods can sit behind there. Of course Adonis is back there, whooping it up with his best friends, Poseidon and Heracles.

Meanwhile, I'm scanning the chariot to see if there's anyone I can sit with. Then I hear, "Oddy! Sit here!" and I realize my best bud is calling me! Yes!!!

But then I realize someone's already sitting next to him. No!!!

"I can't," I say under my breath. "The seat is taken!"

"Oh, I'll take care of that."

OH
MY
GODS!!!!!
It smells like a combination of
FETA CHEESE,
A WET FERRET,
AND FEET!

It's a Feta Ferret Feet Fart! Immediately all the kids nearby get up and squeeze into the other side of the chariot, and I sit down next to the heart of the fart, my best friend . . . Gaseous.

"Wow, that's bad," I say.

"I'm a little gassier than usual this morning," says Gaseous. "I think I'm nervous about starting middle school."

"Sorry," says Gaseous while I check to see if I still have my eyebrows.

"You got a problem, Fire Butt?" says a voice from above. Gaseous and I look up to see Poseidon looming over us, holding his trident in one hand and his nose in the other. He is not pleased.

"No problem," Gaseous replies. "Just a little gas leak, that's all."

"A gas leak?" says Poseidon, turning to the rest of the chariot. "Attention, everyone! We've got a gas leak here. Nobody panic! I've got the situation under control."

Uh-oh.

"I always say, where there's smoke, there's fire—so the best thing to do is put the fire out, am I right?"

"Right!" yell the Gods.

Poseidon takes a deep breath in, and I'm thinking, oh, great—here comes a spitball, but when Poseidon opens his mouth, a *tidal wave* comes out. I try to tell him I'm not on fire, but there's so much cold water being dumped on my head, it sounds like "Ggggll—I'gg luhhg bbl fgglubb!"

When Poseidon finally turns off the waterworks, he announces, "All clear here."

If this is my "new start," I think I'll take the old one!

Gaseous and I are still soggy when we pull up to school. Kids file past us as they leave the chariot—some of them staring, more of them snickering. My brother and Poseidon laugh out loud as they walk by, and my brother shouts, "Cleanup on aisle nine!"

"I thought things would be different this year," I sigh.

"It's probably just the chariot," says Gaseous. "It's not school."

I pull a clump of seaweed out of my hair and exit the chariot. Gaseous turns to Phaethon and says, "Thanks for the ride."

"I have no choice," replies Phaethon. "My father is Helios, the Sun God. He granted me one wish, and I asked to drive his sun chariot across the sky. He said it would be too much for me. I said it wouldn't be, but it was, and I crashed. As punishment, I'm doomed to drive this school chariot for all eternity. . . ."

"Geez, talk about a downer," Gaseous says.

"I hope this year isn't a downer," I say.

"Come on, dude—this is *Mount Olympus Middle*! It's gotta be better than grade school. Doesn't it??"

My flatulent friend might be right. The sun is shining, the sky is bright blue, and as we climb the gleaming marble steps of M.O.M., it sure looks awesome.

From the steps, we can see someone standing by the front door, telling everybody where to go. Wow—it's Ares, the God of war! He's an eighth grader, and a total beast! How cool is that? Ares is welcoming ME to middle school! Gaseous and I mouth, "Oh, boy, is this GREAT!" to each other. Ares smiles, looks us right in the eyes like we're old pals, and says:

"W—w—what?" I stammer.

"This is the Gods' door. You go in there," says Ares, pointing to his left.

"You mean, the door right next to this one?" Gaseous asks.

"Right," says Ares.

“Is that just for today?” I ask.

“Every day,” Ares replies.

Gaseous lets out a tiny *PFFFFFFT.*

“Welcome to middle school,” sneers Ares.

Okay, so let me recap.

Well, that makes sense. Gaseous and I walk through the “other” door, shaking our heads, and head off to our first stop of the day: A.M. Assembly.

CHAPTER 6

When Gaseous and I get to A.M. Assembly, we see the Gods have already grabbed one whole side of the auditorium. We settle in and wait for the assembly to start. Here's the weird thing, though: *no one's talking.* First-day jitters, maybe? Or does something happen to you if you talk? Anyway, the more no one talks, the more no one else talks. It's totally quiet . . . and totally awkward! Seriously, is there anything more uncomfortable than a bunch of kids sitting completely silent in a big room?

"It's too quiet, dude," whispers Gaseous. "It's making me nervous. And when I get nervous, my stomach gets nervous. And when my stomach gets nervous, stuff starts to happen. . . ."

“No no no no no,” I hiss. “Not here! Not now!”

Gaseous lets out one of those long, loud, air-going-out-of-a-balloon farts, and the auditorium goes crazy—*in a bad way.* Girls are screaming, boys are laughing, and everyone is staring . . . at Gaseous and me. It feels like we’re . . .

Just when I think I’m going to have to transfer schools, a super-spooky noise comes from behind the auditorium curtain.

First, there’s a

CREEEEEEEEEEEEEEEEEEEEEEEEEEEAKKKK!!!

followed by an even creepier

OOO*HHHHHHHHHHHHHHHHHHHHHHH!!!*

Then, a skeleton wearing a black robe appears! And speaks!

"OHHHHHHHHHHHHHH!" the skeleton moans. "OHHHHH . . . OHHHHH . . . OHHHH . . . OHH, where did I put my glasses? Silly me, they're right here in my pocket! Silence, please! Good morning. I am Principal Deadipus."

“All right, settle down,” the principal says. “First, I have an important message to all students from the custodial staff: be considerate of others and kindly flush the toilet when you are done!”

“Oh, please—all I said was ‘toilet,’” sighs Deadipus. “Are you really that immature?”

"OHHHH!!!! is right! Now, to those of you who are back, and to those of you who are new, I would like to welcome you all to Mount Olympus Middle School. You are about to embark on a wondrous journey. You will learn and grow and find out who you really are. Some of you already know that you have certain powers. . . ."

"Quiet!" scolds Principal Deadipus. "While others of you might not know . . . yet. But each of you sitting here today has something to offer. And your teachers and I are here to help you discover what that something is. We will help you *discover* and *develop* your powers, whatever they might be. When I think back over my many years of teaching . . ."

"Did you hear that?" I whisper to Gaseous as Principal Deadipus drones on about his youth . . . when dinosaurs were probably around. "They're going to help us find our powers!"

"You think they'll make my farts more powerful?" asks Gaseous.

"I don't think that's possible," I say. "But you can dream!"

"Maybe they'll help you figure out your power, Oddy!" whispers Gaseous. "That would be cool!"

"And there will be one thing more that we ask of you," Principal Deadipus says. "We will ask you to choose a class president. Someone who represents all of you, who embodies Olympus's highest, most glorified ideals. Someone who will be our school's ambassador to the Council of Gods, and Zeus himself!"

"Oh, all right," sighs Deadipus. "Whoever is president will also get lots of cool stuff."

"OH, YEAHHHH!" roars a voice near the front of the auditorium. "I'll take it from here, your honor."

Oh, brother.

That could only be one God talking: my brother.

"With all due respect, Principal Marvelous, I think we all know who should be class president," Adonis says, taking the microphone from Principal Deadipus. "He's got two thumbs and looks like . . . THIS GUY! Thank you, thank you very much!"

The Gods' side of the auditorium erupts like Mount Vesuvius.

"You da God, Adonis!" shouts Poseidon, waving his trident over his head.

"You heard my boy, your excellency!" says Adonis. "That crown is mine!"

"Not so fast, Adonis," replies Deadipus. "This is Greece—the birthplace of *democracy*. There will be an *election*. You'll need an *opponent*."

"I understand, Principal Fabulous," says Adonis. "And you're absolutely right. But really: who would want to run against *me*?"

He's right. Someone would have to be pretty dumb to run against Adonis. Trust me: *he never loses.*

PAINFUL FLASHBACK!

Here's Adonis beating me in crawling . . .

Block building . . .

And blowing bubbles.

FLASH FORWARD TO EQUALLY PAINFUL PRESENT!

"So . . . who *else* wants to run for class president?" asks Principal Deadipus. "Somebody? Anybody?"

No one raises a hand.

"WOO-HOOOOO!" cries Adonis.

"Inside voice, please," says Principal Deadipus, turning his gaze back to the audience. "Students, you have one week to think about it. Should anyone else decide to run, you may inform me at your earliest convenience. That is all."

After Deadipus dismisses the assembly, everyone filters out of the auditorium, Gods first and the rest of us following behind.

"Great—Adonis as class president," says Gaseous under his breath. "That's just what we need."

"I hope somebody else decides to run against him," I say. "But nobody will, because nobody's that *stupid*!"

CHAPTER 8

We walk into the packed, noisy hallway. Ares and Apollo are playing catch with a ball, launching it back and forth. The ball is whizzing through the air, except . . . the ball isn't whizzing—it's wailing! Then I realize the ball isn't a ball. It's a boy!

He's shouting, **"All right, you guys—now I'm really getting mad!"** but with all the noise in the hallway, you can barely hear him. Ares heaves the kid, and he flies high over Apollo's head. He's heading straight at me, like a teeny tiny missile!

I hold up my hand and the kid slams right into it. I barely feel a thing.

He looks up, a little dazed, and says, **"Hi, I'm Puneous. Who are you?"**

"I'm Oddonis. And this is Gaseous."

Then the little guy turns back to Ares and Apollo and shouts, **"Hey, you apes! Now you're in trouble! I've got my boys Oddonis and Gaseous here! It's three against two!"**

"What?" Ares says to Puneous.

"What???" I say to Puneous.

"You heard me! Take a hike before we put a hurtin' on you," Puneous says to Ares.

"WHAT???" Gaseous says to Puneous.

Ares and Apollo start marching toward us.

"Bring it!" screams Puneous.

Before I can explain that we don't even *know* this guy, Ares and Apollo pick the three of us up, stuff us in an open locker, and slam the door shut.

"Come back and fight, you animals!"

"So, how ya doin'?" asks Puneous.

"Umm . . . okay, I guess," I reply.

"I can ride a hamster," says Puneous.

"That's . . . cool."

"How 'bout we knock off the small talk and open the door?" says Gaseous.

"Small talk? Is that some kind of crack?" says Puneous.

"Take it easy, Tiny—I'm just trying to get out of this locker."

"Who you calling *Tiny*?"

"Down, boy," says Gaseous. "Oddy, pull my finger."

"Do I have to?"

"Do *you* have a power that'll open this door?"

"All right, all right," I say. "I'm pulling."

BWWWWWWONNNNNNKKKKK!!!!!

"Stupid Gods! I swear, it's like grade school all over again," says Puneous. **"I bet I was shoved inside every locker at Zorba Elementary."**

"So, how do you like middle school so far?" I ask Gaseous.

"So far, so bad," replies Gaseous.

"Will you guys quit yakkin' already? We gotta get to class!"

As we walk down the hallway, Gaseous and I tell Puneous what life was like at Spartacus Elementary. Actually, Gaseous and I are walking, and Puneous is riding . . . on my shoulder. He says he hitches rides all the time, and most of the time you don't even know he's there.

The three of us step warily into our first class after A.M. Assembly: math. Gaseous and I look at each other and gulp. Math is our worst subject, BY FAR. Math teachers have tried everything to get through to us over the years. One time, they even tried putting us in class with some *slightly younger* students:

In my defense, I haven't always had the greatest math *teachers* in school.

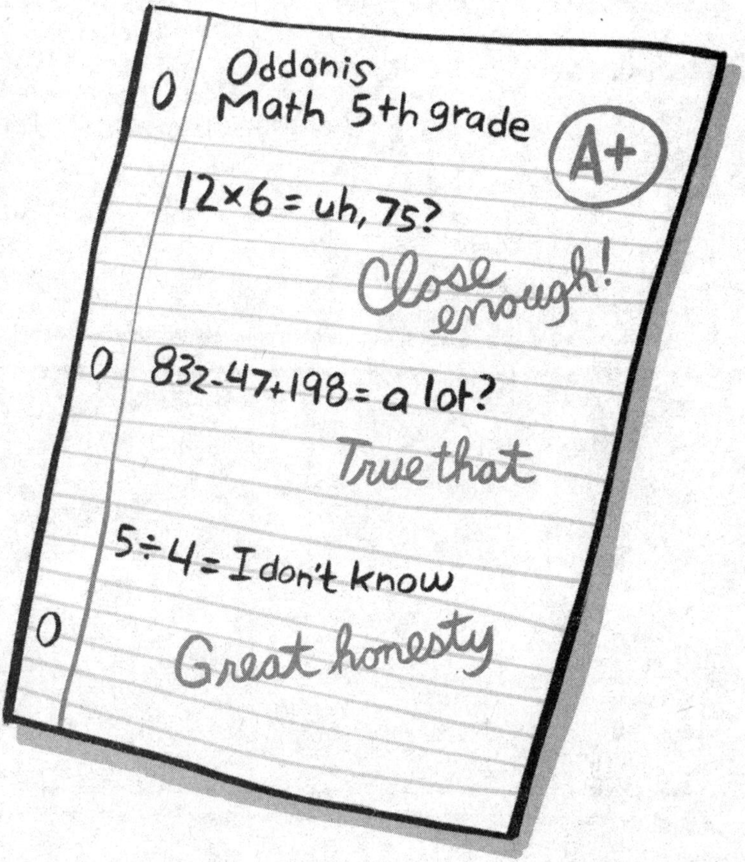

You'd think the teachers on Mount Olympus would be the smartest teachers ever, right? Not so much! Then again, the Gods aren't all brainiacs, either. They do some pretty messed-up stuff!

FAMOUS GOD FAILS!

NARCISSUS
WHY WON'T YOU TALK TO ME, YOU HANDSOME DEVIL, YOU?
SISYPHUS
LITTLE HELP HERE?

ICARUS
I SHOULDA PUT ON SUNSCREEN!

Anyway, I've found that the best way to deal with teachers is to answer their questions super-confidently, like you've never been wrong about anything your whole life. It's always worked before, and I'm hoping it'll work on my new math teacher, Ms. Meticulous.

"Welcome, mathletes!" says Ms. Meticulous. "Pop quiz! Quick! What's sixteen times ten?"

"Two hundred!!!" I shout.

"And what is your name, you eager beaver?"

"Oddonis, ma'am," I reply cockily. "Pretty quick, aren't I?"

"*Very* quick," says Ms. Meticulous. "And *very* WRONG!!!"

See? Worked like a char—wait, what???

"Ms. Meticulous?" says a voice. "The correct answer is one hundred sixty."

"Who said that?" asks Ms. Meticulous.

"I did," says the voice. "Mathena."

"You are correct, Mathena! One hundred sixty it is!"

"I know," says Mathena. "Duh."

Okay, the "Duh" was completely uncalled for!

"Oddonis, you need to get up to speed," says Ms. Meticulous. "I'm going to partner you with Mathena. That should help."

"Ms. Meticulous?" asks Mathena. "Can we maybe do something a little more challenging than multiplication this year?

"What were you thinking of exactly, Mathena?" asks Ms. Meticulous.

"Oh, you know—trigonometry, differential equations, imaginary numbers, things like that."

Imaginary numbers??? Now she's just making stuff up.

"What do you all say?" Ms. Meticulous asks the class.

"Come on, you guys," Mathena pleads. "It'll be SO FUN!"

Mathena gets serious stinkeye from everyone in the room. Then, from the front row, Aphrodite flips back her long, flowing hair and says in her most honeyed voice, "Well, I for one don't think we need *students* telling us what we should be learning, Ms. Meticulous. I'm sure *you* can teach *anything* better than *anybody*! *Right, Mathena?*"

Then she turns around, gives this total death stare to Mathena, and whispers, *"Go pluck a chicken!"* I feel a cold wind blow up my toga.

"Whatever," whispers Mathena. She looks crushed.

"Well, I was going to say we should stick with multiplication," says Ms. Meticulous, "but after Mathena's suggestion, I think I'll make things . . . a little *more challenging* this year."

Mathena lets out a little "Yippee!" but stops when she looks around her.

Like everybody else, I am bummed beyond belief, but I also feel kind of bad for Mathena. Ms. Meticulous tells us to meet our math partners after class, so maybe I can try to cheer Mathena up. I sure know my math skills won't!

CHAPTER 10
ODDONIS'S STEP-BY-STEP GUIDE TO
TALKING TO A GIRL!!!
STEP 1:
Think about talking to a girl.
STEP 2:
Talk yourself out of it!

STEP 3:
Give yourself a pep talk.
IT'S NOT SO HARD! YOU CAN DO IT!
STEP 4:
Make yourself a sandwich.
STEP 5:
Look at yourself in the mirror.
THERE'S NOTHING WRONG WITH YOU!
STEP 6:
Check to see if there's food stuck in your teeth.
STEP 7:
Bounce a ball against a wall for half an hour.
STEP 8:
Give up!

I almost forgot—here's the most important thing about talking to a girl in middle school: *no one else in middle school can know you were talking to a girl.* It's like an unwritten rule. If you talk to a girl, it's got to be TOTALLY SECRET.

"Tough first day," I say to Mathena, while looking off in the complete opposite direction.

"Yup," replies Mathena.

"You . . . uhh . . . sure made me look bad in there!"

"Please. You did that all by yourself."

"Yeah, I guess you're right," I say. "And . . . umm . . . I'm sorry you got the stinkeye from everybody. I mean, I'm not sorry about it, because you kinda deserved it, but I am sorry about it. Like, for you. Not because I wanted you to be happy, because that made me unhappy, but I didn't want you to be sad. So I'm sorry. But I'm not sorry. But I am. Sorry."

"Thanks," Mathena says. "I think."

"You really love math, don't you."

"You figured that out?"

I feel the burn. But I go on.

"No, I mean, you really, really love it."

Mathena finally lifts her head and sighs.

"I do. I love it. I love math. Numbers talk to me, and I talk to them. We understand each other. We help each other. It's like we're friends, and we're playing this beautiful music together. Does that sound weird? Be honest."

"100 percent."

Mathena laughs. "I know," she says. "To you, and everybody else."

"Is that why Aphrodite's so mean to you?" I ask. "Because you're the Goddess of *math*?"

"It's not the math," Mathena says. "The Gods

make fun of me because I'm the Goddess of math and . . . something else."

"What?"

"Promise you won't laugh?"

"I promise."

(I totally don't promise, but I have to say that, right?)

"Poultry?" I say. "You mean, like—"

Just then, a chicken pops his head out of Mathena's backpack.

"It's okay, Clucky—go back to sleep," says Mathena to the chicken, who somehow understands her and slips back down into the backpack. "Yeah. Chickens, ducks, geese, turkeys . . . all poultry."

NOW-I-GET-IT FLASHBACK!

"Aphrodite's been putting me down like that since we were in first grade," says Mathena.

"Wow," I say, "the Gods aren't even nice to other Gods!"

"Not if there's something different about you," Mathena replies. "I can tell you more at lunch, if you want."

"You mean, like, where we'd be sitting at the same table?"

"That's usually how it works."

"Umm, okay, I guess. Lunch it is." Then I realize something: the halls are totally empty. I turn to Mathena and say, "Did you notice there's, like—"

"No one in the halls?" she replies. "Yeah, let's go! We're late!"

CHAPTER 11

Mathena and I hustle down to lunch, huffing and puffing, and throw open the cafeteria doors.

Whew! Not too late! And, from the looks of things, we are in for a treat! Mathena and I scan the room and see the Gods already hunkered down over their delicious-looking lunches. How did they get here so fast?

YUM! Mathena and I skitter up to the end of a huge long line and wait for our share of the goodies.

By the time it's our turn, the Furies . . .

. . . look like they've had just about enough of serving lunch.

"What'll it be, sweetheart?" one says out of the corner of her grouchy mouth.

"Hi," I say. "Could I have the steak?"

"Sorry, kid. Shoulda been here earlier."

"Salmon?"

"Nope."

"Corn on the cob?"

"Nuh-uh."

"Hot fudge sundae?"

"Ha!"

"Well, what *do* you have left?"

"Liver and eggplant stew."

"Liver and eggplant stew?"

"Liver and eggplant stew."

"Got any nectar?"

"Ran out. We have some old hot dog water, though."

Mathena and I look at each other, shake our heads, and sigh.

All I can say is the Furies' stew makes my mom's fiskesuppe look like ambrosia! Mathena and I take our lousy lunches and start looking for somewhere to sit, but there's no place left. We try to grab two spare seats at one of the Gods' tables, but the looks we get are so nasty, they'd even turn Medusa to stone!

Mathena and I realize that if you're not a popular God, don't even *think* of trying to sit with them. We wander around until we reach the back of the cafeteria. We see a table—and it has empty seats! Only problem: the table is right in front of the big, smelly garbage dumpster. Gaseous is sitting there, staring glumly at his steaming bowl of blecchhh.

"I make one pit stop in the bathroom for a quick little toot, and this is what I get: liver and eggplant by the dumpster."

"Mind if we sit down?" I ask.

"Umm . . . no," Gaseous says, "but you do notice you're with a *girl*, right? *The math girl.*"

"Yeah."

"Is she going to sit here, too?"

"That's what I was thinking," she replies.

"Okay. Just know that you're probably violating middle school law."

"Let's live dangerously," replies Mathena.

We put our trays on the table, but as Mathena starts to sit down, we hear:

"Stop right there, sister! Don't move or I'll stab you with my spork!"

"Sorry!" Mathena cries. "I didn't see you!"

"Well, I'm sittin' right here! Open your eyes!"

"I'm really sorry!"

"Yeah, yeah—just watch it next time! Geez!"

It sure would've put a damper on lunch if Mathena had crushed Puneous to death.

"How are we supposed to eat this slop?" grouses Puneous. **"I'd give anything for a chicken nugget!"**

Clucky the chicken pokes his head out of Mathena's backpack and starts squawking.

"WHAT THE—?" screams Puneous.

"Calm down, Clucky," says Mathena. "He didn't mean it."

"Is it 'Bring Your Chicken to School Day'?" asks Gaseous.

"It is when you're the Goddess of math and poultry," I say.

"Hey, birdbrain!" Poseidon shouts from the Gods' table. "Tell that chicken to shut his beak or we'll make a potpie out of him!"

"Oh, go jump in a lake, fish face!" yells Puneous.

Puneous stands tall and proud—or at least proud, until . . .

“Why don’t you pick on somebody your own size?” I bark in Poseidon’s general direction.

Which might not have been such a great idea, because the next thing I know, Poseidon and Heracles are towering over me.

“Heh heh! Who said that?” I sputter. “I—I think he went thataway!”

“Nice try, tough guy,” says Poseidon. “Have a nice trip.”

Heracles slams his mighty fists down on our table, and before I can say, “Where am I going?”—I’m FLYING UP IN THE AIR!

CHAPTER 12

And it's not just me—Gaseous, Puneous, Mathena, and Clucky and Ducky are flying, too!

We look down from up high to see Poseidon sneering at us and Heracles waving goodbye. Man, that dude is *strong*!!!

"Thank you for flying with us today!" yells Poseidon, high-fiving Heracles.

"It could be worse," says Gaseous midair. "He could've thrown us in the dumpster."

Just then, we land with a squishy *THUD* . . . right in the dumpster. The lid slams closed, and we're plunged into inky, stinky darkness.

"Yeah," Mathena replies. "Sure glad he didn't do that."

I look around in the dark. The smell of rotting fish is *everywhere* . . . until I realize there's an old fish stick lodged in my nose. I take it out and hear a voice beside me:

"Who the heck are you?" I ask.

"I'b your classmate," the voice says, "Germes."

After we introduce ourselves, Gaseous asks Germes the question that's on everyone's mind: "WHAT ARE YOU *DOING* HERE???"

"Habbing lunch. Dis is my favorite spod."

"I can see why," says Mathena. "What a beautiful view!"

Germes's voice emerges from the murky depths. He's all stuffed up, so it's hard to understand him.

He sounds sad, too, and that makes me sad. (He's also eating something while he's talking, and that makes me throw up a little in my mouth.)

"I hab to eat here," Germes says gloomily. "If I ate in de cafeteria, de Gods would rip me apard."

"Good poind . . . I mean, point," I say. "They can be pretty ruthless."

"Dey get eberything and we get nothing."

"You said it, Germes!" agrees Puneous.

"They've been doing a number on us forever," says Mathena.

"Cluck cluck cluck!"

"Quack quack quack!"

(Sounds like Clucky and Ducky agree.)

"So what if we're not Gods like dem?" complains Germes. "We're importand, too."

"Right on, bro!" says Gaseous.

"So whad if I like eating garbage out of a dumpster? There's nothing wrong with dat."

"You should've quit while you were ahead, dude," says Gaseous.

"And no offense, Oddonis, but your brudder is a real jerk."

"Oh, he's not as bad as he seems," I say. "He's actually . . . WAY WORSE!"

We all laugh . . . until UFOs (unidentified food objects) fall into our mouths. After we're done coughing and sputtering and spitting, I say, "It's cool to find other guys who get it."

"And girls!" Mathena says.

"Yeah! Here's to new friends!" says Puneous. "Middle school friends!"

We try to high-five, but it's so dark in the dumpster, we end up slapping each other in the face.

"I'd shake on it, but there's leftover pudding on my hand," I tell them. "At least I hope it's leftover pudding."

"Let's shake anyway!" Puneous says. "Anybody got a match so we can see?"

"I do!" replies Gaseous. "Lights, camera, action!"

"My new BFFs," sniffles Germes.

We stare at each other for a really long time. Maybe we should've stayed in the dark. AWKWARD!

"Hib . . . hib . . . hooray," Germes wheezes.

Super-awkward. Finally, Gaseous breaks the silence . . . by breaking wind.

"Oh, NO!" cries Mathena.

"I couldn't help it!" says Gaseous.

"No!" she shrieks. "Gas plus lit match equals—"

BOOM!!!!

WHAM!!!!

Back we land, right at our table, right where we were sitting before.

Germes looks up and mutters hungrily, "Liver and eggpland stew. Yum."

When I get home later, I'm still thinking about my crazy first day at school. I'm barely in the house when I get bowled over by my dog, Trianus.

You've heard of Cerberus, the three-headed dog who guards the gates of the Underworld, right?

My dog is the *stranger* version of that.

What, you were expecting me to have a golden-doodle or something? Sure, Trianus is different, but he's a great dog and I love him. And three butts is no big deal—unless I forget to bring enough bags for his walk!

"Hi, boy!" I say, followed quickly by, "Down, boy! Down! DOWWWN!!!"

Trianus can barely contain himself (it's probably the dumpster gunk!) He's jumping all over me—sniffing and slobbering and licking and barking, his three tails wagging a mile a minute—so I throw him my stinky toga to use as a chew toy and go get changed for supper.

All I've eaten today is that NutriGreek bar and a tiny taste of liver and eggplant stew—and I'm *starving.* On my way down the stairs, though, I immediately lose my appetite when I realize my mom made . . . *smalahove.*

Smalahove is . . . wait for it . . . *boiled sheep's head.* For real!

And Mom serves it on a bed of *mashed rutabagas*.

For some unknown reason, my dad and brother both *love* smalahove. I used to think there was something wrong with me, until Gaseous came to dinner—ONCE—and said afterward . . .

My dad and Adonis are already at the table, salivating. And they're not just psyched about the smalahove—they're also stoked about Adonis's announcement at school.

"So, you're running for class president?" asks my dad.

"You know it, Pops!" says Adonis.

"Just remember, son—anyone can run. Only one God can *win*."

"Yes, sir! And I will! I just need an opponent . . . that I can CRUSH!"

"That's my boy! You're a born leader!"

Then Dad looks at me.

"And you're . . . uh . . . er . . . I'm sure you've got some talent, too, Oddonis!"

I know he's joking (he *is* joking, right?), but inside I'm thinking, "Why is Adonis a born leader and I'm not?" Then I remember the time I was supposed to lead a goat in the fourth grade play. That did not go well.

I'm feeling a little bad about myself when my mom leans over and whispers in my ear, "I *know* you were born to do great things!"

Awww! Thanks, Mom!

"Now, have some more smalahove."

Ewww! No thanks, Mom!

CHAPTER 14

You know how stuff your mom or dad says can sometimes stay with you for a long, long time? That's what my dad's "born leader" comment does to me. I think about it all night and all through the morning at school. I'm still thinking about it when I'm standing in the hallway with Gaseous after lunch. I'm also thinking about that goat butting me in the behind. Then, out of nowhere, I get kicked hard . . . right in the butt!

"OWWW!" I scream. I turn to Gaseous and ask, "Was that the goat???"

"I don't know what goat you're talking about," replies Gaseous. "But you do have a KICK ME sign on the back of your toga. Someone must've stuck it on you when we got off the chariot this morning."

"I think I know who."

"You okay, dude?" asks Gaseous. "You seem kinda out of it!"

"I do?"

"Yeah, you didn't even notice *the hall monitor*."

"What hall—" And then I notice. "Oh, wow," I say. "What *is* that?"

"I am the Sphinx!" the creature roars. "I monitor these halls, and I tell you where to go!"

"We're good, thanks!" Gaseous says as he and I start tiptoeing away.

"You shall not pass!" thunders the Sphinx. "Not until you answer a riddle!"

Gaseous and I start to sweat. Neither of us is

good under pressure, especially when the stakes are this high.

1. Get answer wrong.
2. Get eaten by the Sphinx.

"Answer me this," roars the Sphinx. "Whose really smart, incredibly handsome brother would make an *awesome* class president?"

"Ha ha. Very funny."

"Busted!" laughs the Sphinx. "I got you guys so bad! You should've seen your faces!"

Gaseous and I are still shaking our heads when we meet Puneous and Germes out near the quad.

It's another perfect day on Mount Olympus. We find a gorgeous spot on the lawn, and are about to sit down when we hear:

"HALT!"

Artemis (and her bow and arrows) stands in our way.

“No sitting on the grass,” Artemis says. “Gods only.”

“Gods only?” says Mathena. “You canNOT be serious!”

“This area is the Gods’ grass,” says Artemis. She’s VERY serious.

Another day, another diss. If only I had the power to do something about it.

But I don't have any powers. And no one's going to argue with Artemis, because

1. She's an eighth grader, and everyone knows you don't mess with eighth graders, and
2. She's got a bow and arrows, and everyone knows those can really hurt!

We step away from "the Gods' grass" and park ourselves on a lovely patch of . . . pavement.

"De Gods' grass," sulks Germes. "Now I'b seen eberything!"

We sit on the concrete and commiserate. We all agree middle school isn't exactly what we thought it would be. And it's not going to get better anytime soon, because our next class . . . is *gym*.

CHAPTER 15

One big change in middle school is now we have to wear uniforms in gym class. And let's just say those uniforms look a little better on the Gods . . .

. . . than they do on us.

Our gym teacher, Coach Gluteus Maximus, blows his whistle and gathers us in a circle.

"All right, troops, today we're going to play a little game called Capture the Fleece," says the coach. "At each end of the field is a golden fleece, just like the one Jason brought back from Colchis. Your job is to capture the fleece and return it to the center of the field before your opponents do. Now, how do you junior Argonauts want to pick teams?"

"Gods against everyone else!" yells my brother.

"And their ugly ducklings!" sneers Aphrodite, death-staring at Mathena, Clucky, and Ducky.

"I don't like our chances," says Mathena.

"Who cares?" says Gaseous. "I'd rather have our team than a bunch of snobby Gods!"

Even though it feels like we're getting ready for our own funeral, we make a game plan. We decide to keep Germes back by our goal, defending our fleece. (We figure no one will want to get within ten feet of him!) The rest of us line up and wait for the whistle.

Gluteus Maximus stands at the center of the field and says, "Team Gods, are you ready?"

"Ready, Coach!" says Adonis.

"And Team . . . uhhh. What's your team's name?" the coach asks me.

"Umm . . . gee . . . I don't know," I reply. "Uhh, Team—"

"Team Odds, are you ready?"

"Ready, Coach," I answer, knowing that we're really . . . NOT.

The coach blows his whistle, and we Odds start running. Only the Gods . . . aren't! They don't move a muscle. They're just standing there, like . . .

My brother and Poseidon are chatting away, like they're waiting for the chariot. As Mathena dashes past Artemis and Aphrodite, Artemis says, "Wow, look at Mathena go!"

Aphrodite replies, "Yeah, she's *poultry in motion*! Hahahahahahaha!"

Mathena ignores the insult and keeps going. We all do. Gaseous and Puneous and I are getting close to the golden fleece, but then we see who's guarding it: Heracles! Mr. Muscles sees us coming toward him, and then he does the craziest thing: he yawns a huge yawn and lies down on the field to take a nap!

"What the heck is going on here???" cries Puneous.

"Maybe they're afraid of us!" says Gaseous.

"I seriously doubt that!" I say.

"Less talking, more running!" Mathena says. "Get that fleece!"

I grab the golden fleece, and our whole team takes off toward the center of the field. And still the Gods are just standing there! This is unbelievable! We might actually win something! We might beat the Gods! Just a little farther and . . .

"Team Odds is the winner!" declares Gluteus Maximus.

Team Odds goes nuts. We're jumping up and down, hugging each other. It's like we just won the Olympics! I'm so happy that I even hug Germes!

"Wow," says Adonis. "Congratulations. You guys were amazing out there."

"Thanks," I say, still trying to catch my breath.

"In your face!" screams Puneous at the Gods.

"Yeah, you definitely deserve it," says Adonis. "But just a quick question: are you sure that's the golden fleece?"

"Sure we're sure!" says Gaseous. "Look at it!"

"I don't know," says Poseidon. "You might want to turn it over."

I flip the fleece over, and staring me right in the face is a . . . SKUNK!!!

The skunk sprays Team Odds from the tops of our heads down to our toes. WE. STINK.

"Mmmm," murmurs Germes. "Dat's lovely!"

Meanwhile, the Gods are rolling on the field laughing. As my brother holds up the real golden fleece and hands it to Gluteus Maximus, even the *coach* is chuckling.

"Did you honestly think you could beat us?" asks Adonis. "Come on! Wake up, weirdos!" And the Gods march off the field, triumphant once again.

I look over at my dejected and defeated teammates, and think, *If only I had a power, any power . . .*

But I've got nothing. I feel terrible . . . but I feel worse for my friends. My brother's words are ringing in my ears. Then it hits me—just like one of my dad's lightning bolts!

Adonis is right—I *do* need to wake up. I turn to everyone and say, "That's it. I'm sick of this. I've got to do something. I'm mad as Hades, and I'm not going to take it anymore!"

"Oh, yeah?" asks Gaseous. "What are you going to do?"

"I'll probably get crushed, but I don't care. I have to try."

"Try what?" asks Mathena.

"Listen, you guys—I might not have a power, but

I want to get *US* some power."

"And how the heck are you going to do that?" asks Puneous.

"I'll tell you how: I'm running for class president."

Silence hangs over the field. Then the ground starts rumbling, and shaking, until there's a colossal clap of Gaseous's *thunder from down under.*

"YEAHHHH!!!" screams Gaseous. "I give that a twenty-one-toot salute!"

Now we're covered in skunk stink *and* Gaseous stink! But that doesn't seem to be affecting my friends. "We can be proud to be odd!" I say. And one by one, everyone lifts up their heads and joins in.

GO WITH ODD!
ODD SPEED!
ODD ALMIGHDY!
ODD BLESS US, EVERY-ONE!
M.O.M.
IN ODD WE TRUST!!

CHAPTER 16

After gym class, we Odds proudly march into Principal Deadipus's office to tell him I'm running for president. It's a pretty short meeting.

When I get home after school, Trianus is OUT OF HIS MIND over my odor.

I jump in the shower, scrub off the skunk, wrap myself in a towel . . . and nearly have a heart attack.

"AAAAHHHH!!!" I scream.

"Well?" asks my dad. "What do you have to say for yourself?"

"Umm . . . sorry for the smell?"

"Your brother tells me there's someone *else* running for class president."

Uh-oh.

"Oddonis, I'm very disappointed in you," Dad says. "I thought we had an understanding."

"I guess I didn't understand the understanding you thought I understood," I say. "Understand?"

He doesn't. Now Dad tries a different tactic: warm and fuzzy. Not really his strong suit.

"Oddy, we talked about this. Leadership is your brother's thing, and . . . well . . . uhh . . . ummm . . . you have your thing."

"He does have a thing," says Adonis. "It's called *embarrassing ME*!"

"Enough!" the Great God growls at Adonis. "You need to spend less time *whining*, and more time *winning*!"

Adonis turns beet red with shame. Can't say I feel bad for him!

"And as for you, Oddonis . . ."

I feel bad for me, though!

"All I'm saying is, certain positions should be left

to those with the right skill set. I wouldn't want you to embarrass *yourself*—or this family."

Hmmm.

"Just think about what I said, Oddonis." And Zeus disappears into the mist.

"You heard him. Don't mess with success, *Brometheus*," Adonis hisses. "And I wasn't whining!" Then he slips into the mist, too . . . and walks right into the sink.

I straggle into my bedroom, throw on a clean toga, and sit down on my bed. I'm stung by what my dad said. Does he really think that little of me? I guess he does. Liquid starts streaming down from my eyes. Must be the steam.

Then I hear a knock at my door.

"Oddy, honey? Can I come in?"

"Sure, Mom."

My mom sits down next to me and puts her arm around my shoulder.

"You okay?" she says.

"Yeah. Are you here to yell at me, too?"

"What? No, kjaere—I would never! You're my elskling! My skatt sötnos!"

That's Norwegian, in case you're wondering. Mom's either saying I'm her dear one or her rolling pin—I can't remember which—but right now it sure sounds hyggelig . . . I mean, nice.

"You heard what Dad said?" I ask her.

"I did," Mom replies. "Your father sees things a certain way. But that doesn't mean he's always right. And it certainly doesn't mean he can't learn."

"Who am I kidding, Mom?" I say. "Even if Dad was okay with it, how can I possibly beat Adonis?"

"I think you can do anything you set your mind to."

"You really believe that?"

"I do."

Moms are the best, aren't they?

"Now, come down for supper, snuppa. I roasted a reindeer!"

Hmmm. Guess you have to take the good with the bad!

CHAPTER 17

The next day I'm actually feeling pretty good about myself. And even though my brother keeps giving me the deep freeze and his friends try to make me rethink my decision . . .

I'm actually kind of . . . happy. Weird! And I'm super-excited for this afternoon, because after school, we're having our first Team Odds campaign meeting. We decide to meet at the one place we know Adonis and his gang won't disturb us: the library. (Not cool enough for them, I guess.) The library's closed, but Ajax, the school janitor, lets us in. He's really nice, and stronger than dirt™!

My campaign manager, Mathena, calls the meeting to order. I'm so psyched to hear what she has to say!

"This is a disaster," says Mathena.

Okay, maybe I'm not so psyched to hear what she has to say!

"Here's our problem: nobody knows who you are! I took a poll and asked students, 'What do you think about Oddonis?' Nearly 27 percent of them thought I was saying 'Adonis,' and 72 percent thought I was saying 'A dentist'—which made your negatives go up even more! But fear not."

Mathena pulls out some kind of clicker, and a screen drops down from the ceiling. She clicks again, and a presentation appears with the title:

"I have done extensive polling and research," begins Mathena. "Thanks to the MAGIC of mathematical data analysis, I have targeted numerous preferences of likely voters, as well as what influences those voters most, and I have devised a formula that I believe gives Oddonis the best chance to win this election." Mathena clicks, and the screen flashes:

NAME GAME + PET PARADE = VICTORY

"If we focus our energies on these two factors, my projections show that, with a sampling size of approximately 64 percent, assuming a margin of error of plus or minus three points, and random poll fluctuations within a range of 8.5 to 12.5 percent—"

"**Get to the point, will ya?**" yells Puneous.

"We just might win this thing!" says Mathena. "Now, if you'll please take out the binders I've placed in all of your backpacks, I'll explain my methodology . . . and our mission."

I have no idea what Mathena is talking about, but I don't care. I can't believe I'm saying this, but could it be that . . . math is my friend?

"Math is your BEST FRIEND!" Mathena shrieks.

How did she do that???

Meanwhile, math sure isn't being my friend in Ms. Meticulous's class.

I can't think about that now. We've got a campaign to run! First up on Mathena's list is Name Game. She says we need to get my name out there in new and creative ways. Of course, the first thing we all think of is . . . POSTERS! Right? We've been making posters *forever.* What is it with posters anyway? Why do teachers assign so many of them? Whatever the reason, posters are NOT what Mathena is thinking. She says posters are old school, and too easily "doctored." I totally get what she means:

So, posters are out. Mathena wants us to "think outside the box" and uses words like "branding" and "media saturation" and "market penetration." It makes about as much sense to me as "random poll fluctuations," but who am I to argue? If it weren't for Mathena, my campaign would be posters . . . and prayers.

Believe it or not, our first big idea comes from Germes. Mathena wants us to walk around school with a megaphone, chanting pro-Oddonis stuff, but Germes suggests we ride instead—by souping up our old lunchtime pal: the garbage dumpster!

"It's got wheels, and it smells heabenly," says Germes.

Germes says he can build a platform on top of the dumpster that we can all stand on. Cool! The bigger problem is how to actually make the thing move. Sure, it's got wheels, but it weighs a ton! We'll need a serious push to get it going. Then I remember something I've been trying really hard to forget:

EXPLOSIVE FLASHBACK!

"Germes," I suggest, "if we hook Gaseous up to the back of the dumpster, couldn't we use his caboose for a ca-*boost*?"

"Can't see why nod!" replies Germes.

"You need gas?" shouts Gaseous. "Bring on the beans!"

The next day, we're ready for launch. Gaseous finishes fueling up with one last can of baked beans, and we strap him and his "engine" to the back of the dolled-up dumpster. Mathena and I climb up to the platform, Germes grabs his makeshift steering wheel, and Puneous gets ready to light the rump rocket.

"This is the worst job EVER!" moans Puneous.

"Gentlemen, start your engines!" shouts Mathena. "Three, two, one—BLAST OFF!"

Gaseous erupts, the dumpster shakes, and slowly but surely we begin to lurch forward. We're actually moving!

"We need more power!" yells Germes.

"I'm givin' her all she's got, Captain!" replies Puneous, shoving another spoonful of beans into Gaseous's mouth.

As the dumpster rolls out of the cafeteria, the crowd that's gathered begins to laugh (that's bad!)

and then begins to cheer (that's good!). I wave to them as Mathena picks up a megaphone and sings out:

I'm Oddonis, and I did *NOT* approve those messages! But they seem to be working! Students are lining up to watch as we pass by, and everyone is pointing and smiling! The dumpster is picking up speed . . . and it looks like my campaign is, too—until I hear Puneous scream.

"Incoming! Bogeys at five o'clock!"

What the heck does that mean?

"Looks like we'be got company!" shouts Germes.

I turn my head to see Adonis, Poseidon, and Heracles in a chariot, closing fast! My brother has this mad look in his eye as he waves to the crowd, and Poseidon hollers to Heracles, "Time to take out the trash!"

Heracles leans out of the moving chariot and, with *one finger,* begins to lift the dumpster up in the air!

"What do we do???" I cry out to Germes. "He's going to dump us!"

"Nod if we dump him first!" says Germes. "Bombs away!" He grabs a lever next to the steering wheel and pulls hard. One side of the dumpster drops down and empties its putrid payload . . . right on Adonis's chariot!

O . . . M . . . Gs! We're clean and dry up on our

platform, while Adonis and friends are coated with stinky slimy slop! (The cafeteria's "Tuna Surprise" never looked better!)

"Good riddance to bad rubbish!" calls Puneous.

We leave the grimy Gods behind, finish our triumphant around-the-school tour, and park the dumpstermobile right back in our spot.

"And that's how you play the Name Game!" Mathena exclaims. "Next up . . ."

CHAPTER 19

. . . Pet Parade!

"My statistical analysis indicates that 98.2 percent of students love anything to do with animals," Mathena says. "Numbers-wise, it's totally off the charts!"

"LOVE IT!" says Gaseous. "What do we do?"

"We bring our precious pets to school for Oddonis's Pet Parade. Kids will eat it up!"

"What if my pet is a little lacking in the precious department?" I ask.

"Then dress him or her up in some darling outfit, and nobody will know the difference!" replies Mathena. "Just . . . think . . . cute!"

With the day of the election coming up quickly, we've got to move fast. We plan the Pet Parade for the following day, and I head home to see what I can do to darling up my dog (and hide his tri-heinie).

"What are we going to do with you?" I say to Trianus. I'm starting to get worried when, out of nowhere, a memory flash hits me: BABY BUMBLE!

SWEET BUT EMBARRASSING FLASHBACK!

When Adonis was little, he had a little doll that he named Baby Bumble. He LOVED Baby Bumble. He fed Baby Bumble, he bathed Baby Bumble, he diapered Baby Bumble, and he burped Baby Bumble! He took Baby Bumble *everywhere*. He even had a little stroller that he pushed Baby Bumble in.

My dad wasn't a fan of Baby Bumble. He'd give Adonis every toy sword, spear, club, lightning bolt, helmet, and suit of armor he could find. He'd get him stuffed dragons, stuffed centaurs, even a stuffed cyclops—but nothing could compete with Baby Bumble.

Finally Dad put his foot down and told Adonis that *real Gods* didn't play with babies. Then he banished Baby Bumble to the attic. Adonis was crushed, Mom was furious—but Dad wouldn't budge, and after a while, Baby Bumble was replaced by those toy swords and stuffed dragons. I kinda think the nicest parts of Adonis went up to that attic with Baby Bumble and stayed there. And that's where I go now—to bring down Baby Bumble's baby clothes and stroller!

AWWW!!! Isn't he SO CUTE??? There's even a box of toy diapers in Baby Bumble's stroller, so I grab three and tape them to Trianus's three . . . *bum*bles.

The next day, everyone smuggles their pets into school in their backpacks, and the team meets in the quad during free period to set things up. It's Pet Parade time! After I introduce Trianus (who's *totally* into his baby bonnet, stroller, and diapers, btw), Gaseous takes his turn.

LOOK WHO I BROUGHT! THE SKUNK FROM THE "CAPTURE THE FLEECE" GAME. I ADOPTED HIM!
HIS NAME IS "AROMUS"!
AROMUS IS CUDE, BUT CHECK OUT MY PEDS: HARRY AND HELGA HEAD LICE!
I HAVE TWO PETS!
FIRST, SAY HELLO TO MY TRUSTY CARRIER PIGEON, PENELOPE!

NOW STAND BACK, EVERYBODY, BECAUSE MY OTHER PET IS A LITTLE INTIMIDATING. DON'T BE AFRAID, THOUGH. THIS IS... BRUISER!
HE'S A MONSTER!
HE'S ADORABLE!
HMPH!
DON'T WORRY, PENELOPE, SO ARE YOU!
OKAY, YOU GUYS, I HOPE YOU LIKE MY PET. SAY "HELLO" TO MY CUDDLY WUDDLY BUDDY-

Well, that's our Pet Parade lineup! It's a menagerie of misfits, but I like it. I just hope the rest of my classmates like it, too!

My classmates don't like the Pet Parade—they LOVE the Pet Parade!!! It's a humongous hit! Kids are cooing and cuddling the animals, totally digging this zero-stress activity in the middle of the school day. The teachers enjoy it, too! Ms. Meticulous kisses Eggasus's . . . shell?

. . . and Principal Deadipus lets Bruiser crawl around inside his head.

Even the Furies find a friend!

Seeing everyone so happy gives me an awesome idea. "If I'm elected class president," I announce, "I will ask that pets be allowed in school before every test to help us all CHILL OUT!"

"I'll second that!" Deadipus says, rubbing Bruiser on his itty-bitty head.

The crowd cheers. The noise attracts my brother and his posse. Adonis surveys the scene, frowns, and says, "Talk about a sorry safari! This is the stupidest, most pathetic excuse for a—" Then Adonis stops. He stares at Trianus in his stroller, gasps, and whimpers, "Baby Bumble?"

Adonis's eyes start to well up with tears, until Poseidon sneers, "Baby *who*?" Then Aphrodite asks, "Adonis . . . are you . . . *crying*?"

Adonis immediately gathers himself, wipes his eyes, and replies, "What? Crying? No way! It's . . . it's just a stupid mutt in a baby bonnet! I must be allergic to him!"

Hmmm.

"These animals are so lame!" Adonis shouts. "They don't even *do* anything!" Adonis whispers to Poseidon and Heracles, and the two of them run off. Then Adonis turns to the crowd and says, "You want to see something *really* special? Feast your eyes on this! Look! Up in the sky! It's a bird! It's a mane! It's . . . Pegasus!"

The students turn away from the Pet Parade to see the majestic white horse soaring high up in the blue, its magnificent wings flapping powerfully in the wind. Poseidon holds Pegasus's reins, and Heracles sits behind Poseidon carrying some sort of metal canister. The crowd is OOOHHING . . . and AAAHHING . . . and *FORGETTING* all about the Pet Parade.

"Holy Helios!" cries Gaseous, "he's skywriting, too!"

Sure enough, white smoke starts trailing from behind Pegasus. Everyone is riveted, staring up at the sky, waiting to see what the message will be. Slowly the words start to form.

“NOOOOOO!!!!” wails my brother. “YOU IDIOT! IT’S THE OTHER WAY AROUND! Adonis jumps up and down, waves his arms at Heracles, and screams, “IT’S SUPPOSED TO SAY, ‘*ADONIS* RULES, *ODDONIS* DROOLS!’” But Heracles is too high up to hear him. He smiles, waves back, and gives Adonis a big thumbs-up.

“FIX IT, YOU DUMMY!” shrieks Adonis. “FIX IIIIIIIIITTT!!!”

Too late. Pegasus flies off. The deed is done.

“ODDONIS IS THE ONE WHO DROOLS!” bawls Adonis. He stamps his feet like a toddler who needs a time-out. “*HE* DROOLS! *I* don’t drool! I *NEVER* DROOL! I rule! I RULE!”

The crowd begins to scatter, giggling at the spectacle they just witnessed. Adonis sees Team Oddonis smiling, then marches up to me and whines, “It’s not fair! Tell them! Tell them all—*YOU* drool! *I* rule!”

“You know what they say, brother,” I reply. “*Drool* unto others as you would have them *drool* unto you.”

“Yeah,” laughs Mathena. “That’s the Golden *Drool*!”

The Odds are definitely looking up! (Meanwhile, my math grade is definitely looking down!)

I'll deal with that later—too busy! Besides, everyone (except Mathena) seems to be struggling, so I'm not alone. After another confusing math class, my team makes a plan to talk over our next campaign moves at lunch.

But when we get to the cafeteria (late again!), we see Adonis and his gang standing near the front of the food line, handing out free cups of nectar to all the kids who were too late for the good food—and now have to eat today's other offering: Mystery Macaroni. (More like *Misery* Macaroni, from the looks on the kids' faces.) And oh, brother, Adonis is milking that nectar for all it's worth.

"Step right up! Drinks are on me!" he crows as the grateful crowd lines up for a syrupy slurp.

Team Oddonis watches from our usual place in the back of the lunch line.

"Sorry you all missed the filet mignon," says Adonis. "I hope I can make things a little better with some sweet, sweet nectar. No need to thank me, though. It's just me being . . . me."

"What a windbag," Gaseous mutters. "And I should know!"

"But wait—that's not all!" says Adonis. "There's more!"

"You've done so much already, Adonis!" fawns Aphrodite as she pours cups of nectar from a fountain. "How can you do any more?"

"Yes!" echoes Artemis, handing out the cups. "Aren't you tired?"

"I'm tired of this!" Puneous grumbles as he picks up his teeny tray of macaroni.

"Sure. I'm tired." Adonis nods, lowering his voice to a solemn, self-serving whisper. "But I can't help it. I'm a giver."

Oh, give me a break.

"And I won't stop giving, because that's who I am. And that is why I am announcing a promise to all of you."

"No way!" shouts Poseidon.

"Yes way!" Adonis replies. "I hereby pledge to you that my campaign team and I will provide *free math homework help* to anyone who needs it."

An excited murmur spreads through the crowd. They can't believe their ears. Neither can Mathena.

"That's right! Your math homework will be done fast, and done right—guaranteed!"

The murmur turns manic. Everyone goes bonkers. Even *I'm* wondering how I can get in on this deal! No!!! *Must . . . resist . . . free . . . math . . . homework . . . help!*

"Just put your name on the bulletin board, and I, or a member of my tremendous team, will set up a time to meet with you. And remember: I'm doing this because I care."

"ADONIS ROCKS!" screams Heracles. "CROWD SURF!!!"

As he passes us, Adonis turns his head to Gaseous and me and says, "No tutoring for you two. You're beyond help!" Then he orders his entourage to whisk him away, and they do . . . right into a chandelier.

"OWWW! Stupid chandelier!"

"We're toast," sighs Puneous.

"He's the one who's toast," seethes Mathena. "Homework help? Done right—guaranteed? Now he's gone too far!!! NOBODY messes with my math!" Mathena turns to the team and says, "Listen up, you guys. I'm calling an emergency campaign meeting after school. I'm counting on you, so you better be there. Four o'clock—at the Olympic Diner!"

The Olympic Diner is our favorite snack shop on Mount Olympus, and it's run by one of the sweetest and oddest guys we know: Fryonysus.

Fryonysus is the best cook in all of Mount Olympus. He found the perfect job to fit his *unique* power! Fryonysus isn't just fast—and sure, having *twenty arms* helps—but I swear, he can make *anything.* He's also a really nice guy, with tons of great stories. And because Fryonysus isn't like everybody else, he totally gets us.

The Olympic Diner is in the middle of the Mount Olympus Mall. You have to pass by a bunch of places before you get there—Pandora's Boxes, Build-a-Centaur Workshop, Vesuvius's Secret, The Homer

Depot, Togas 'Я' Us, Namba Nectar, Sandal Shoppe, the Ambrosia Factory, and the Nike store. But once you're there, it feels like home.

"Hey, all my faves are here—what are the odds?" says Fryonysus, giving us all high fives . . . at the same time! "I've got your table set up—but I'm warning you, Mathena's been here awhile, and I haven't seen her this mad since she missed one question on a quiz last year!"

Gaseous, Puneous, Germes, and I join Mathena at a corner booth.

"Math proofs," snarls Mathena. "Whenever I get tense, I do math to calm myself down."

"You do math for relaxation?" asks Gaseous. "That so does not add up."

"You know what really doesn't add up?" she snaps. "Adonis doing everyone's homework for them!"

"Something's definitely fishy," I say.

"**Yeah, I smell a rat,**" chimes in Puneous.

"Dat mighd be me," says Germes.

"I smell pancakes!" says Gaseous.

"Couldn't help overhearing, Oddy," says Fryonysus. "But is your brother that smart?"

"Sure, Adonis is smart," I reply. "But—"

"But he certainly isn't smart enough to do everyone's homework!" thunders Mathena. "*I* can't even do that! Okay, I *can*, but I *wouldn't*!"

"Adonis says his whole team will do it," scoffs Puneous. **"That means Aphrodite, and Poseidon, and . . . Heracles! HERACLES! He thinks algebra is a guy named Al Gebra!"**

"Yeah, there were only twelve labors of Heracles because he couldn't count any higher!" laughs Gaseous.

"Enough!" screams Mathena. "We've got to focus! This is important!"

"Calm down," Gaseous says. "What's got you so worked up?"

"You guys don't get it," says Mathena. "I *love* math, and I work really hard! If everyone gets their homework handed to them, they're not working for it. And they're not learning to love *math*—they're just learning to love getting the best *grade* in math. We need to get to the bottom of this, and fast!"

"Mathena's right," I say. "*And* if we can figure out how Adonis is cheating and catch him in the act, he's sure to lose!"

"How are we going to do dat?" asks Germes.

"Beats me," I sigh. "Adonis won't breathe a word to me, and it's not like we can sneak inside his pocket and follow him around all day."

"We can't," says Puneous. "But I can!"

The next morning, Puneous knocks on my bedroom window, and the two of us sneak into my brother's room while he's in the shower. Puneous hides inside Adonis's backpack, and Operation Dinky Drop is on! (And no, we did NOT tell Puneous the name!)

All day long, we worry about our knee-high spy. We're assuming no news is good news, but can't rule out *other possibilities*:

The waiting is torture. By the time dinner rolls around, I still haven't heard from Puneous. I'm a nervous wreck!

"You've hardly touched your moose nuggets, Oddonis," Mom says.

"I'm just not hungry, Mom," I reply.

"Then pass them here, doofus," says Adonis. "I loves me some moosie!"

"Finish your dinner, Oddonis," barks my dad. "That's an order."

Three nuggets left. There is *no way* I'm going to finish.

"Dad, I'm really not—"

"There you go!" says Mom. "Good eating!"

I look down, and the nuggets are gone. Whaaaaat?

"Well, lookie there," says Dad. "See? I guess you *were* hungry after all!"

I take one more peek in my lap, and there, belly full, wiping his mouth with my napkin, is Puneous!

Buuuurrrrppp!

"I beg your pardon?" says Dad. "How about an 'Excuse me'?"

"Right! Excuse me!" I say giddily. "Great moose, Mom! Can I be excused?"

I stuff Puneous in my pocket, leap from the table, and hustle him into my bedroom. I'm so relieved, I want to hug him—but I don't want to smush him!

"We were so worried, Puneous! Thank Gods you're okay!"

"Your family eats moose, dude!" says Puneous. **"Kinda wrong . . . but kinda delicious, too!"**

"So what'd you find out?"

"TONS, but I gotta get home before my parents freak out!" says Puneous. **"You'll have my full written report in the morning! TTYL!"**

Puneous whistles, and his pigeon, Penelope, appears at my window. Puneous jumps onto Penelope's back like he's mounting a stallion, and flies off.

"Home, Penelope!" cries Puneous. **"Yee-haaaaa!"**

"Puneous," I chuckle, "you are a small wonder."

CHAPTER 24

Bright and early, I hear a *tap-tap-tap* at my window. Penelope Pigeon is there, with a rolled-up piece of paper strapped to her little leg. I gently remove the paper, roll it out, and . . . can't see a thing. The writing is so small! I get out my magnifying glass, and this is what I find:

CLASSIFIED
CONFIDENTIAL
TOP SECRET!
INTELLIGENCE REPORT
GATHERED AND SUBMITTED
FOR YOUR APPROVAL
BY UNDERCOVER AGENT PUNEOUS

9:04 A.M. SUCCESSFULLY EMBEDDED IN ADONIS'S BACKPACK. COMMENCING OPERATION DANGER DROP. (THAT IS THE NAME, RIGHT?)

10:46 A.M. ADONIS STOPS STUDENT IN HALL AND ASKS FOR HIS "WALKING PASS." STUDENT SAYS HE'S NEVER HEARD OF A WALKING PASS BEFORE. ADONIS TELLS HIM HE'LL GIVE HIM ONE TOMORROW FOR FREE. STUDENT THANKS ADONIS AND LEAVES. ADONIS LAUGHS, WHISPERS, "ANOTHER VOTE FOR ME!" AND WALKS RIGHT INTO A LOCKER DOOR. SAYS, "OWWW! STUPID LOCKER!"

11:59 A.M. WAITING FOR NOON LUNCH BELL TO FINALLY SEE HOW GODS GET DOWN TO LUNCH SO FAST.

12:00 P.M. IN CAFETERIA! HOW DID THAT HAPPEN???

12:05 P.M. AMAZING LUNCH. ALL-YOU-CAN-EAT SHRIMP AND STRAWBERRY SHORTCAKE. (WORST. FOOD NAMES. EVER!!!) OH, AND THE OTHER CHOICE ON TODAY'S MENU? LIVERWURST SANDWICHES AND STEWED PRUNES! UNBELIEVABLE!!!

1:03 P.M. LATIN CLASS. (LATIN JUST AS BORING INSIDE BACKPACK, BTW.)

I PEEK THROUGH MESH POCKET TO SEE IF ADONIS IS DRAWING ANYTHING INCRIMINATING, BUT THE ONLY DOODLES I SEE ARE

2:12 P.M. ADONIS TELLS APOLLO, "I'LL GIVE YOU THE GOODS AFTER SCHOOL. MEET ME AT THE SPA."

2:17 P.M. WHAT ARE "THE GOODS"? AND WHAT IS "THE SPA"?

3:14 P.M. ADONIS, POSEIDON, AND HERACLES WALK TOGETHER TO GYM LOCKER ROOM. THIS IS "THE SPA"? A BUNCH OF

STALLS THAT SMELL LIKE WET TOWELS AND B.O.??? THEY STOP IN FRONT OF A LOCKER, UNLOCK THE COMBINATION, AND SUDDENLY, WE'RE IN . . . AN ACTUAL SPA!

HOW CAN THIS BE??? I AM OUTRAGED!!!

3:22 P.M. APOLLO, STRETCHED OUT ON A RECLINER IN A FLUFFY WHITE ROBE, SAYS TO ADONIS, "CHOP CHOP, CHIEF! I'VE GOT A TUTORING SESSION AT FOUR O'CLOCK!" ADONIS REPLIES, "HOLD YOUR TOGA—I GOT IT RIGHT HERE." THEN

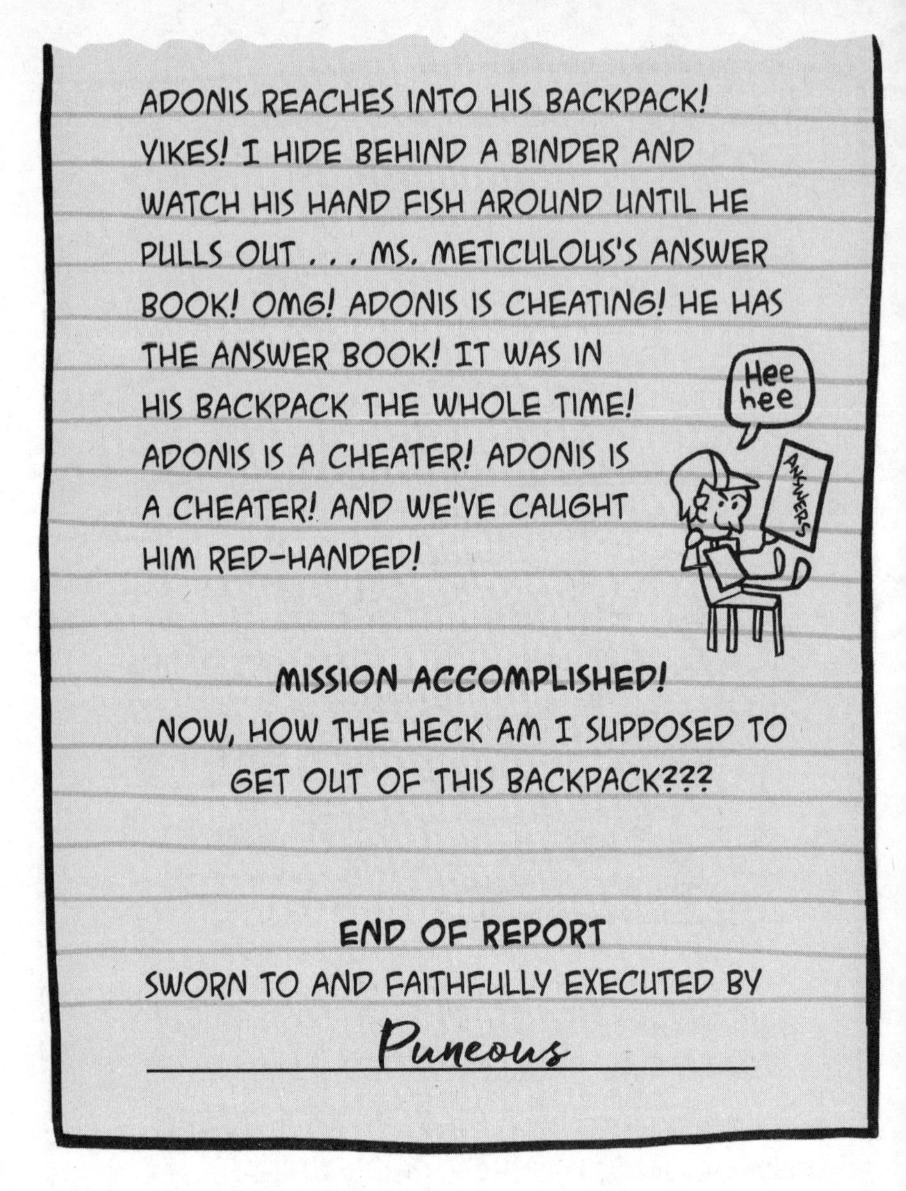

Wow. I can't believe it. I mean, I *can,* but I *can't.* I'm shocked, and dazed, and thrilled . . . but I'm also a little sick to my stomach. My brother is lying to everybody, and I have the evidence *right here*. What should I do? Think, Oddy, think! What would Adonis do if he were in my shoes?

Turn me in.

And that's *exactly* what I'm going to do.

EXTRA! EXTRA! READ ALL ABOUT IT!
The Mount Olympus Middle Monitor
BAD-ONIS! GOD CAUGHT CHEATING!
Anonymous Tip From Unidentified Pigeon
Presidential Debate Today - What Will Adonis Say?
Oddonis Surges To 12% In Poll
Students Must Redo ALL Math Homework
Mathena Excited

CHAPTER 25

It's unbelievable. The whole school is buzzing, and everyone is pointing the finger . . . at *my brother*! For the first time ever, Adonis is in hot water for something he did. Trust me: he NEVER gets blamed! For anything!!!

ANGRY CHILDHOOD MEMORY!

Now, because of all the extra math homework, everyone's ticked off at my brother. And the timing couldn't be worse for Adonis, because today is the presidential debate! Three podiums are set up at the agora in the quad—one for me, one for Adonis, and one for the moderator, Principal Deadipus. I'm pretty nervous, but because of this cheating scandal, my team thinks the only way I can lose is if my toga falls off!

"We will start alphabetically," says Deadipus. "Adonis, you will be allowed to make a brief opening statement. In light of your recent actions, what do you have to say for yourself?"

Adonis takes a scroll of paper from his toga, clears his throat, and speaks.

"Principal Deadipus, fellow classmates, dear friends," Adonis utters softly. "Four score and seven hours ago, a date that will live in infamy, I looked out over the mountaintop and I could see that we have nothing to fear but fear itself, and I asked myself not what my school could do for me, but what I could do for my school!

"Let me start again," says Adonis. "And let me speak . . . from my heart. When I embarked on this lonely quest to be your class president, I had one

goal: to see everyone enjoy the same benefits, the same successes, and the same joys that I get from Mount Olympus Middle School every single day.

"So, when I *just happened* to find Ms. Meticulous's answer book, I was left with a choice. Return the answers, and watch my classmates suffer through their math homework—"

"Suffer? *Suffer?*" hisses Mathena. "There's no suffering in math! There's delight, and discovery, and a merger of mind and material in a great cosmic union—"

"Oh, please!" whispers Puneous. "Take it somewhere else!"

"Or," says Adonis, "keep the answers and *give* them—freely, with *zero* expectation of reward—to anyone who needed them, so that they too might enjoy the stellar grades that I have been lucky enough to receive." Adonis bows his head. "I see now that I was wrong."

A worshipful hush falls over the audience. Adonis has them hook, line, and sinker.

"I . . . am a God," says Adonis. "It's true. I can't deny it. And I'm sure that before this happened, most of you thought I could do no wrong."

UMM . . . CAN I OBJECT???

"But you know what? I've learned something. Maybe it's okay to make mistakes—because that makes me more like . . . *all of you*."

Adonis squeezes his eyes really hard, and squeezes them again, and again, and again, until finally a single, tiny tear rolls down his cheek.

"I'm sorry. I was blinded by my *deep love* for my fellow students, and I made a bad choice. I only hope that all of you can . . . *sniff* . . . see it in your hearts . . . *sniff sniff* . . . to forgive me . . . *sniff sniff sniff*. Thank you."

Except for the Team Odds row, there isn't a dry eye in the house. Even Deadipus—who I'm pretty sure doesn't even *have* eyes—wipes a tear from his skull.

"My oh my, that . . . *sniff sniff* . . . was quite an opening statement," Principal Deadipus blubbers, and turns to me. "Oddonis, would you care to respond?"

You bet I would! But first—my conscience wants a word with me!

I know what I need to do. I'm shaking. I'm sweating. But I'm ready. After all, the truth is on my side, right?

"My fellow students," I say, "we must not ignore the facts. My opponent—"

"Oh, wait," Adonis interrupts. "Just one more thing, Principal Deadipus."

"You've had your turn, Adonis," says Principal Deadipus.

"I know, sir," says Adonis. "But if I may, this is kind of important."

"All right, Adonis," replies Deadipus. "Go ahead."

"I happened to be looking over the school's bylaws this morning, and I noticed something. In order to be eligible to run for class president, a student cannot be failing any of his or her classes, right?"

"That is correct, Adonis," replies Principal Deadipus. "Why?"

"Well, sir," says Adonis. "Sadly, it has come to my attention that Oddonis, my opponent, is currently failing math."

"Oddonis," says Principal Deadipus, "is this true?"

It feels like every eye in the entire world is staring at me.

I swallow hard. "Yes, sir. It's true."

The Mount Olympus Middle Monitor
FRAUD-ONIS OUT!
Oddonis Removed From Class President Ballot
New Poll: Voters Say "We Believe Adonis"
Deadipus: Cheating Scandal Is Now "A Dead Issue"
"This Stinks!" Says Gaseous
"THAT Stinks" Says Kid Standing Next To Gaseous
READ EVEN MORE ABOUT IT!

CHAPTER 26

I'm such a Dumb-donis. I knew what was happening. I knew I was having trouble. But I was too embarrassed to ask for help. I even had Mathena as my math partner! I guess I hoped it would all just magically go away. And now the election has gone away . . . and my F is still right here!

Meanwhile, Team Odds is crushed—*and* disappointed. Even Gaseous is!

"I would've helped you, dude," he says. "Then you'd have a D like me!"

I know I let my friends down. They believed in me, and I failed them. I'm so ashamed, I feel like crawling under a rock. (I actually try to, but when I turn the rock over, I find Germes under there eating a toadstool.)

The rest of the day is a miserable blur. After school, I decide to hike up Mount Olympus to get away from everything and clear my head. I climb up, and up, until I reach a shimmering emerald lake. I sit down on a rock by the lake and hang my head. I'm so mad at myself, I feel like screaming. Then I realize I can scream as loud as I want, so I do.

"AAARRRGGGGHHHH! I'M SO STUPID!!!"

Then I hear, **"I'M SO STUPID, STUPID, STUPID . . ."**

"I'M SUCH A BONEHEAD!"

" . . . BONEHEAD, BONEHEAD, BONEHEAD . . ."

And so, because I'm a kid and *that's what we do*, I yell, "ECHO!!!"

"ECHO, ECHO, ECHO . . ."

"Yes, yes, yes?" says a woman's voice. **"Can I help you, you, you . . . ?"**

And there, standing next to me, is a beautiful nymph.

"What the—"

"What the, the, the," she says . . . IN MY VOICE!!!

"Who are you?" I ask.

"Who are you, you, you?" she asks.

"I'm Oddonis, Oddonis, Oddonis."

"Adonis, Adonis, Adonis?" she asks.

"No. O*dd*onis, O*dd*onis, O*dd*onis."

"A dentist, a dentist, a dentist?"

"NO! ODDONIS! ODDONIS! ODDONIS!"

"No need to shout! I am Echo, Echo, Echo. I am an Oread—one of the mountain nymphs, nymphs, nymphs."

"You're *Echo*? Holy cow, cow, cow."

"Why did you call for me, me, me?" Echo asks.

"Oh, I didn't mean to—I was just messing around, around, around."

"Well, thanks a lot! I was taking a nap, nap, nap!"

"Sorry, sorry, sorry!"

"So why are you here, here, here?" Echo asks.

"I had to get away, Echo. I messed up bad, bad, bad."

I tell Echo everything that's happened. All she does is echo what I'm saying, but somehow it feels better getting it off my chest.

"But now what do I do, do, do?" I say.

"Hee hee," giggles Echo. **"You said doo-doo, doo-doo, doo-doo."**

"Did not! Cut it out, will ya, ya, ya?" I say. "I'm in trouble here, and it's up to ME to do something about it!"

"It's up to YOU to do something about it, it, it."

"I'M the one who screwed up, and I'M the only one who can make it right."

"YOU'RE the one who screwed up, and YOU'RE the only one who can make it right, right, right."

"You know you're not really echoing me anymore, anymore, anymore," I say.

"Hey, I just call 'em like I hear 'em, 'em, 'em," says Echo.

Hmmm.

"Got it. Thanks for your help, Echo, Echo, Echo," I say. "I don't know how I'm going to do it, but at least now I know what I have to do, do, do."

"Hee hee! You said 'doo-doo' again! Good luck, a dentist, a dentist, a dentist!"

CHAPTER 27

I haven't figured anything out by the next day, and I'm not ready to face anybody. There's only one place in the whole school I can hide out: the bathroom.

I'm sitting in a stall, feeling sorry for myself, when I hear the door open. Whoever it is who just walked in goes to the sink to wash their hands, and all of a sudden I notice these moths flying around my head! Weird! Then whoever it is starts talking out loud to no one in particular.

"You know," he says, "I hear that if somebody passes just *one test,* they can lift their grade from an F to a D or a C almost immediately. Isn't that something? And all they'd have to do is ask their teacher. . . ."

Whaaaat? I leap from my seat and burst through the stall door, but no one is there. I run out into the hallway (no, I didn't wash my hands first—give me a break!), but the halls are completely empty.

I race up to Ms. Meticulous's room and ask her if I can take a makeup test.

"Technically you can, Oddonis," Ms. Meticulous says meticulously, "but you're going to need help studying for it. *A LOT* of help."

Then I think about my friends.

"I'll have to figure it out myself, Ms. Meticulous."

"What about your math partner?"

"Not likely. I'll be surprised if she ever speaks to me again."

"Oh, yeah?" says a voice from the door. "Shows how much you know."

"Well, well," says Ms. Meticulous. "Oddonis, it seems you know your friends as well as you know your math!"

"I'll help you, Oddy," Mathena says. "But you've got to play by my rules."

"Whatever you say!"

"Will you promise to study like you've never studied before?"

"Yes!"

"Will you devote your mind, body and soul to the pursuit of math excellence?"

"Yes!"

"Will you recognize math as the most wondrous miracle the world has ever known?"

"You can say that again!" snorts Ms. Meticulous.

Hmmm.

"No miracles necessary," says Mathena. "If you work hard, and do what I tell you to do, this test will be easy as pi."

"We'll see about that," says Ms. Meticulous.

As we walk out of Ms. Meticulous's room, I ask Mathena, "Why are you doing this?"

"Because you're terrible at math. Duh."

Still not a "Duh" fan!

"No, I mean—why are you helping me after I let you all down?"

"Because," Mathena says, "we need you."

"You do?"

"Yup," replies Mathena. "The whole team agrees. We need you, warts and all."

"How'd you know about my warts???" I ask. "I got rid of most of them!!!"

"I wasn't talking about *actual warts*," says Mathena.

"Oh."

"Ew."

"They're not where you can see them."

"TMI!"

"Most of them are on my—"

"STOP!" Mathena screams. "What I meant was, just be yourself!"

"Okay," I say. "You can count on me."

"I know," she replies. "Now, let's cut the mush and do some math!"

All right! Cue the "Working Hard" music, please!

Okay, how about some "Working Harder" music!

Uhhh . . . got any "This Is Harder Than I Thought It Was Going To Be" music?

Whoa—give me that "OMG, It's Happening" music!

Now, hit me with some "By George, I Think He's Got It" music!

I'm ready . . . I think. I'll take the test first thing tomorrow morning, before the election assembly. If I pass, I think I can get back on the ballot just in time! It could be a big day!

CHAPTER 30

"Big day today, right?" Dad says . . . *to my brother.*

"Are you kidding? It's gonna be THE BOMB!" replies Adonis as he shoves a Norwegian pancake into his mouth. "No one else decided to run for president, so unless someone steps up, Principal Deadipus said it's all mine. We're gonna have the most flamdiggity, bizonkers, hootie hoo, shoobadoop, off the heezy, perkilatin election of ALL TIIIIIIIME!!!"

"Is that good?" Mom asks Dad.

"I have no idea," says Dad.

"*Good???* It's the best!" gloats Adonis.

"It would have been best if you had an opponent," Dad says. "Being handed something isn't the same as winning it, son."

"I had an opponent, Dad—but he couldn't pass math!"

I look up, but keep my mouth shut.

"How *is* math going, Oddy?" asks Mom.

"Okay, I guess," I say. "I'm trying."

"That's all anyone can ask," says Dad.

"So all he has to do is *try*?" asks Adonis. "That's real fair!"

"It's different for you," replies Dad. "You are a God."

"And what's Oddonis?" asks Mom.

Dad hesitates, then says, "Oddonis . . . is . . . trying."

Hmmm.

"That's true, Dad," I say. "But unlike Adonis, I'm trying because I want to, not because you're telling me to!" I grab my stuff and march out of the kitchen.

Wow! I can't believe I just said that . . . TO MY DAD! How did I do that??? I've NEVER been able to do that!!! I'm just about to leave the house when my mom stops me.

"I'm sorry, Oddy. He didn't mean it. . . ."

"Don't you get tired of apologizing for him, Mom? Maybe Dad's the one who should be sorry."

"It's complicated."

"No, it's not. He expects Adonis to win. He *wants* Adonis to win."

"Oddy—"

"It's okay, Mom. I get it. That's the way it is, and always will be."

As I walk outside and step onto the chariot, I am NOT a happy camper. All I can say is, nobody better get in my way!

"I'm Phaethon, your driver. My father is Helios, the Sun God. He granted me one wish, and I asked to drive his sun chariot across the—"

"I KNOW!!!"

CHAPTER 31

When I get to school, I'm still rattled by all that stuff with my family. I trudge up the front steps and stare at the ELECTION DAY TODAY! banners hanging over the entrance. I take a deep breath and walk through the doors. Hey, it couldn't be any worse than standing out here!

Or could it?

It's like a bad dream! But then I hear my pal Gaseous's voice:

"Let's go, dude! Time to make some magic!"

I look up and there, waiting for me, is Team Odds.

"You mean, 'Time to make some *math*-gic!'" Mathena says.

Okay then—I guess it's time for some "Moment of Truth" music, too!

And last but not least . . . play that funky "He Did It" music!

Okay, it's a C-. What'd you expect, a miracle? But the main thing is:

I'M BACK, BABY!!!

CHAPTER 32

There's no time to lose! We all sprint down the halls toward the auditorium, where A.M. Assembly is about to start, like, any minute now! It's kind of crazy, but my team is even more excited about me passing than I am! So is Ms. Meticulous! She runs ahead to show Principal Deadipus my test score, so he can put me back on the ballot.

Meanwhile, I head backstage to wait with my brother. Basically, Adonis and I will each give a speech saying why we want to be class president. Then, after I'm booed or laughed off the stage, everyone will vote. The votes will be counted right then and there . . . and Adonis will win. But I'll cry over that milk when I spill it!

When I walk into the little room off the side of the stage where my brother and I are supposed to sit before we go on, I find Adonis checking himself out in a mirror.

"This is so frustrating!" Adonis blurts out.

"What is?" I ask, wishing I hadn't.

"I keep trying to find something wrong with my face, but I can't! I'm just too perfect!"

"Yeah, it must be *so tough* being you," I reply sarcastically.

"You have no idea how hard it is," Adonis replies.

"Yeah, right."

"I'm serious. You heard Dad this morning. All you have to do is try; I have to be perfect *all the time*. He always wants . . . more."

Hmmm.

"You should thank the Gods you'll never have that problem, Oddy."

Wow. How about that? I never thought my brother had *any* problems!

"What are you doing here anyway?" Adonis asks. "Come to wish me luck?"

"Not exactly. I passed my math test, so I'm back on the ballot."

Adonis sighs, stands, shakes his too-perfect hair and smiles his too-perfect smile, and gets ready to take the stage.

"Well," says Adonis, "I hate to break it to you, *brotato chip,* but I think you're too late. Now, if you'll excuse me, I need to go out there and seal the deal." Then he points his finger at my chest and adds, "Hey, you've got something on your toga." And for probably the *gazillionth* time since we were little, I look down . . . and Adonis slaps me in the face. "Ha ha—made you look!"

I can't see anything from where I'm sitting offstage, but I can hear the thunderous ovation my brother gets when Deadipus introduces him.

"So . . . how you all doing out there?" Adonis roars to the audience.

The audience roars back.

"Sweet!!!" replies Adonis. "Hey, how'd you like all that FREE Adonis swag out front?"

Another roar.

"And how about that nectar fountain in the cafeteria? AWESOME, right??? So here's my next question: who got that for you?"

"You!" screams the crowd.

"I can't hear you. Who?"

"YOU!"

"WHO???"

"YOU!!!!!"

"Right. And who's the only one who's going to *keep* getting it for you?"

"YOU!!!!!"

"Exactly. If you like *stuff,* I'm your God. So get out there and vote for godliness. Vote for perfection. Vote for the Greek ideal. Vote for . . . ME! Thank you! Thank you very much!"

The roar to end all roars.

Adonis soaks up the adoration, takes a bow, and struts off the stage . . . right into a steel batten attached to a counterweight rigging system.

"OWWW!!! Stupid steel batten attached to a counterweight rigging system!"

So now it's my turn. Yikes! As Principal Deadipus explains to the audience why I'm back on the ballot, I make a list of my usual pre-speech symptoms:

Then I realize I forgot one thing on my pre-speech list: MY SPEECH! Mathena told me to write something, in case I passed the math test—and to practice reading it out loud. Well, I didn't get around to writing anything, but I *sort of* practiced in front of a mirror.

All the practice in the world wouldn't have prepared me for this, though. The room is boiling. The lights are blinding. The silence is terrifying. I don't even know how to begin. Then I remember Gaseous once telling me that great speakers always start with a joke.

"Hi," I say, "I'm Oddonis. So . . . umm . . . what do you call a guitar player who just looked at Medusa?" Nobody answers, so I say, "A *rock star.*"

More silence.

"Get it? 'Cause . . . y'know . . . Medusa . . . uhh . . . turns everyone to stone . . . and umm . . . stones are another word for rocks?"

"Heh heh," I stammer. "Pretty quiet out there. Heh heh."

Poseidon, sitting in the front row, yawns loudly.

"Anyhoo." I hem and haw. "I sure am happy to be back on the ballot, and I promise to do lots of great stuff if I'm elected class president. How about no homework for a year?"

Still quiet out there. I don't think they're buying it—probably because Adonis wouldn't even promise that!

"Maybe we'll start with no homework for a day. Heh heh."

THIS IS NOT GOING WELL. I decide to be a little more Adonis-y. That seems to work with this crowd.

"Okay, but you guys will see—it'll be AWESOME! AMAZING! STUPENDOUS! Why? Because I SAY SO!!! Right? RIGHT???"

The audience stirs. Finally, some noise! Unfortunately, it's the sound of everyone's butts moving around in their seats. Now I'm really sweating. My head is perspiring so much that a large pool of sweat is starting to form on the podium. I look down and I see my reflection in it. I stop, and I stare. There I am. Me. With my sweaty head, and my goofy smile, and my crazy hair. But you know what I suddenly realize? I'm okay with it. I maybe even *like* what I see in that sweat pond. And that makes me smile.

"Let me start over," I say to everyone. "Look, you guys—I think we all know that I'm not my brother. It's silly for me to try to be like him, or make promises like him, or say I'll get you a bunch of stuff like him. 'Cause I can't. In case you haven't noticed, I'm O*dd*onis, not Adonis. That's right. I'm odd. There:

I said it. I'm odd. I'm *odder* than odd! I'm so odd, I don't even know what my special power is . . . other than being odd!"

It's still quiet, but now it feels like a different kind of quiet: it's quiet because they're listening.

CHAPTER 34

"So why did I run for class president?" I say. "Beats me! Only a total oddball would run against Adonis, and that's what I am. But guess what? So are a lot of us. And even if you don't *think* you're odd, I'll bet each and every one of you has some weird thing."

"But who cares? Those quirky things are part of what makes each of us . . . *US*! If you ask me, anybody who says they're perfect either doesn't get it, or they're lying about their own little oddities."

"I'm pretty perfect!" yells my brother from offstage. "Just sayin'!"

"Well, I'm not," I say. "And I don't want to hide my oddness anymore, or pretend it isn't there. I've tried to do that for too long. It doesn't work. So listen up, all you freaks, geeks, dweebs, dorks, nerds, and hidden weirdos out there, and hear this: I'm ODD . . . and I LIKE IT!"

A loud murmur runs through the crowd, until it's broken by an even louder

BWWWOOOOOOOONNNKKKKKKKKK!!!!

I'd know that *bwonk* anywhere. Gaseous stands up, with his head (and tail) held high.

"That's my salute to strangeness, homeys! *I'm* ODD, and *I* LIKE IT!"

Mathena gets up next, hugging her flock. "I love math, and I *really* love poultry, and I don't care what anybody thinks. I'm ODD and I LIKE IT!"

Puneous and Germes follow Mathena. Puneous screams, **"Good things come in small packages!"** and Germes adds, "We all *hab* germs, and we all *need* germs!" Then together they say, "We're ODD and WE LIKE IT!"

"And here's what I like most," I say. "My friends. They stuck with me till the very end. And really, isn't that what all of us are looking for? Someone

who gets us . . . who understands . . . who forgives us when we mess up . . . who will be there no matter what . . . someone who listens . . . someone who *cares*. That's what I want to be as your class president—not just for some of you, but for all of you. I might not be cool, and I might not be able to give you a foam finger or a nectar fountain, but I promise I'll give you my time, my respect, and my friendship. And there's nothing odd about that. Thank you."

CHAPTER 35

It's quiet all over again. No one's talking. There's no sound. Even that kid in class who can't stop bouncing his leg up and down isn't moving a muscle.

From the back of the auditorium, I hear one very soft, very tentative clap, followed by another clap, and another one, and another one. Then, like raindrops on a pond that ripple out further and further, the clapping grows and grows until it seems like the whole school is clapping, the whole auditorium is shaking, and the whole world is saying, "We hear you."

Principal Deadipus comes up to me at the podium, shakes my hand, and whispers in my ear, "In all my eight hundred years, I've never heard a

better speech. Well done, my boy."

Then the mouse that lives in his eyehole pops his head out to say congratulations!

Deadipus turns to the student body and announces, "That concludes A.M. Assembly, and the campaign for class president. Voting will begin immediately. Line up in an orderly fashion to receive your ballots—single file. That is all."

Before I can say, "What just happened?"—my friends jump onstage and wrap me up in a big bear hug.

"Oddy, you were awesome up there!" screams Gaseous.

"**YOU KILLED IT!**" yells Puneous.

"Nice speech," adds Mathena. "But mathematically speaking, I'm not sure it matters. My polls aren't showing an uptick in your numbers."

"Who cares?" I reply. "I got through it, I said what I wanted to say, and my toga didn't fall off! That's a win-win-win!"

Germes's eyes are red and watery, and he looks overcome with emotion. So sweet! He motions me to come closer to him. I do, and Germes leans over and whispers in my ear, "I hab da flu—and I mighd throw up."

We all walk off the stage and out into the hallway. It's wild—kids who never even noticed me before are patting me on the back and giving me

I never get

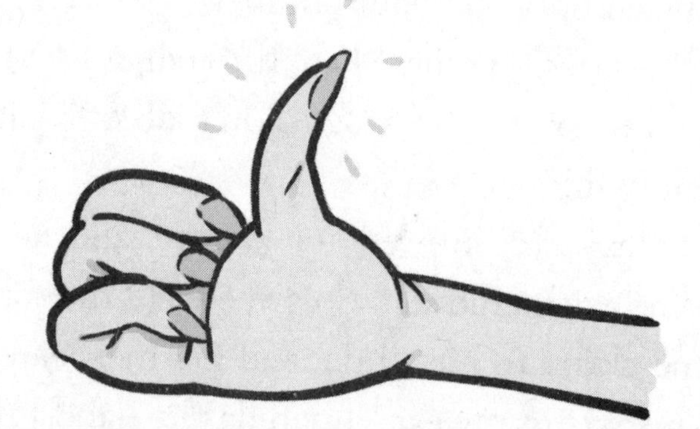

I'm a

guy!

Then I get pushed, back and forth, by a bunch of jock-y Gods—I think it's their way of showing affection, maybe? I'm flying this way and that, whooping it up, until I run headfirst into a brick wall. Only the wall has legs . . . and arms . . . and Heracles's face. My brother stands beside him.

"Having fun?" says Adonis.

"I guess," I say woozily. "Except for the concussion."

"I always said you had a screw loose," replies Adonis. "Now it's official."

"What do you want?" I ask.

"It's time to announce the winner . . . I mean, to announce *ME*," says Adonis. "Deadly says the candidates have to walk in together before he reveals the results. Some hot air about the wonder of democracy or something."

"I'll show you some hot air," grumbles Gaseous.

"Put a sock in it, King Toot," replies Adonis. Then he turns to me and says, "Let's go, little bro—I've got a victory party to get to!"

Adonis and I walk back into the auditorium together and take our places on the stage. Adonis makes sure he stands where the light hits him perfectly—and nudges me into a dead spot where the lights don't reach. One good thing is now I can see. One bad thing is now I can see *MOM AND DAD* in the back of the audience! How long have they been there? (Also, king of the whole world, and this is what he's doing on a Friday morning? Really?!?)

Principal Deadipus steps up to the podium, holding a piece of paper in his bony hand. He pulls two large water bugs out from under his robe and lays them on the paper to hold it down. Ingenious, yet disgusting!

"The votes have been tallied, and the winner is—"

"Thank you, your eminence," interrupts my brother. "And thank you all! Smart move, gotta say. Good call by you—"

Principal Deadipus clears his throat. "Excuse me,

Adonis, but the winner is . . . no one."

"No one? What do you mean, *no one*?" sneers Adonis.

"I mean, no one," he replies. "Because it's a tie."

"A WHAT????"

"You heard me: *a tie*. And we have one further complication: not everyone voted."

"Are you KIDDING ME???"

"I most decidedly am not," says Deadipus. "We are one vote short."

"Who didn't vote???" asks Adonis. "What halfwit, dimwit, nitwit, blockheaded nincompoop DIDN'T BOTHER TO VOTE???"

I take a step out of the dark, and into the light, and smile. "Umm . . . me."

CHAPTER 36

All Hades breaks loose. I have no clue what's happening, because it's so LOUD and there's so much talking and screaming and laughing and crying going on. All I know is that I'm being mobbed by Team Odds. Mathena is hugging me and Gaseous is butt trumpeting and Puneous is screaming, "DON'T STEP ON ME!"

A blizzard of white confetti is falling from the sky, and I think, That's weird, where did we get confetti? I look up to see Germes jumping up and down on the podium and realize that it's not confetti—it's his dandruff!

But who cares? Let it snow! The next thing I know, I'm being hoisted up in the air and paraded around the stage. Now that I'm up above the crowd, I can see the entire auditorium, and I notice my brother, surrounded by his friends, sobbing buckets. Wow, I don't think I've seen Adonis cry like this since Baby Bumble was put up in the attic. Oh, no—here comes my conscience again!

"I'm so torn!" I moan.

"Do you need a new toga, dude?" Gaseous asks, "I have extras, in case I . . . y'know . . . release the hounds."

Release the hounds? Ewww!!!

Meanwhile, Principal Deadipus—after almost getting knocked down in all the hullabaloo and brouhaha (okay, those words mean the same thing, but they're fun to say)—makes his way through the hubbub and hurly-burly (more fun!) and steps back up to the microphone. Team Oddonis stands on one side and Team Adonis the other.

"Well, now that we've regained some semblance of composure," says Deadipus, "Oddonis, I believe I have something for you. Your ballot." He hands me a piece of paper, and I stare at the choice in front of me.

Holy cow, this is actually happening. I can't believe it. All I have to do is—

"Wait," says my brother. "Wait just one second."

Oh, no. Not again.

What is he up to now???

"I've got something to say," Adonis announces. "I am not going to take this lying down. No sir. No way. I am a GOD . . . and . . . as a GOD . . . an all-seeing, all-knowing, all-powerful . . . GOD . . . I need to say . . . I need to say that . . . I have never . . . I repeat, NEVER . . . seen a better candidate than my brother Oddonis."

Whaaaaaaaaaaat?

Adonis sighs deeply and says to me, "Oddy, I didn't think you could do it, but you did: you actually beat me, fair and square. You, and your goofy team. I can't believe it. SERIOUSLY, I CANNOT BELIEVE IT. But it's true. You're a winner. And you always have been. Congratulations, brother—you deserve it."

I totally don't trust this. But everyone's watching, so I can't very well refuse him. So I finally reach out and shake my brother's hand and . . . and . . . and . . . nothing happens! No bone crushers! No ripping my arm out of its socket! He doesn't even pull me in for a noogie!

"Time for you to cast your ballot . . . Mr. President," says Adonis.

I look out at my classmates, at all the Gods and Goddesses sitting on one side of the room and all the non-Gods sitting on the other. I see my brother's crestfallen crew, and my blissed-out band of misfits, and I make my choice. I pick up my ballot, hold it up in the air, and tear it in half.

"Call me Mr. *Co-President,* Mr. Co-President," I say to Adonis.

Now it's Adonis's turn to be shocked. "Are you serious??? But—why?"

"Yeah—WHY???" asks Gaseous.

"Because we need to stop being so divided, and start working together," I say. "Besides, Adonis might be the worst brother in the world," I add, "but he's *my* worst brother in the world—and I think he's learned something."

"HE'S NOT THE ONLY ONE WHO'S LEARNED SOMETHING," a voice booms from the back of the auditorium. Oh my Gods, it's my dad! He and Mom come forward and join Adonis and me on stage. "I heard every word you said, Oddonis," Dad says. "And I'm very impressed. I'm afraid I haven't been very fair to you, or your friends. And I'm . . . sorry."

Sure, the "sorry" part wasn't very loud, but still—he said it!

"And I want you all to know that Oddonis was right when he said that nobody's perfect. Well, *I am,* of course, but the rest of you aren't."

Mom gives Dad some STUPENDOUS stinkeye.

"All right, all right: I never clip my toenails at night, vegetables canNOT touch the rest of my food, and I *always* jump into bed so witches won't grab my ankles. Are you happy now?"

Wow—did not see that coming!

"Hear me now," declares Mighty Zeus, "as King of the Gods, and Ruler of Mount Olympus, I hereby proclaim: no matter how different they might be, the ODDS are all GODS in my book."

The auditorium EXPLODES with applause. My dad puts his hand on my shoulder and smiles. Then my mom grabs me and gives me one of her famous Scandinavian squeeeeezes.

"See, snuppa?" Mom says. "I was right—*twice.* I told you: everyone can learn."

"You were right," I say. "But what else were you right about?"

"Don't you remember? I said you could do anything you set your mind to!"

"Thanks, Mom. But there's one thing I still don't get."

"And what's that, kjaere?"

"If I'm a God, what am I a God *of*? What's my special power?"

"Sweetie," replies Mom, "it was right in front of you the whole time. Your power is helping others find theirs."

"YES!!!" cheer the Odd Gods.

"And that, my son," says Dad, "is what a born leader does."

Hmmm.

I am the great God Oddonis, and I couldn't have dreamed of a better ending. And I can't wait to see what happens next!

Adonis asked for a recount.